Tales from

MEMORY CREEK RANCH

Susan K. Marlow

CONTENTS

ACKNOWLEDGMENTS

Many Circle C Milestones fans have asked if there are future Milestones books in the works. There is good news and bad news. No full-length novels are planned as sequels to the Milestones.

However, this short-story collection covers some of the more interesting events during the "lost" courtship (between chapters 25 and 26 of *Courageous Love*) and also includes stories from Andi and Riley's first year together on their new ranch, Memory Creek, that was deeded over to them by the Carter family as a wedding gift.

I am grateful for the contributions of the faithful readers of Andi's blog, **CircleCAdventures.blogspot.com**. Readers had fun offering many ideas for naming Andi and Riley's new ranch. They voted for their favorite cover. Their input has been invaluable.

A special thank-you goes to Ellen Senechal, who filled in as my ghost-writer for numerous Andi's Journal posts. I took some of those blog posts, rewrote them, and transformed them into the stories for this collection. The posts I chose eventually became "Temporary Teacher," "The Shooting Lesson," "Lamb Trouble," and "Andi Had a Little Lamb."

I also used ideas from Abbi Grooms ("Overgrown Kitty"), Sadie Saller ("The Shooting Lesson"), and Patience Yeh ("Yosemite Nightmare"). Thanks, ladies!

Tales from Memory Creek Ranch is not published by Kregel Publications. Any errors you encounter are my own. Feel free to email me corrections. They can be fixed in future printings. Contact me at **CircleCAdventures@gmail.com**.

Susan K. Marlow

Part 1: Courtship 1885-1886

A VERY SPECIAL SPOT

CIRCLE C RANCH, CALIFORNIA, FALL 1885

I think Riley and I are kindred spirits. He can sense when I need to get away. He just knows. After making a bobble out of the new coffee cake recipe Melinda insisted that I should try to bake, I just want to get out of here!

Chapter 1

Riley Prescott barreled through the back door and straight into the Carters' kitchen. He didn't bother to knock. "Andi!"

"What's wrong?" Andi dropped the pan of crumbs that had started out as a coffeecake. "Is Shasta all right?"

She swiped at a dark tangle with a floury hand. Her heart pounded. The memory of Taffy's accident and unexpected passing two years ago lay buried just under the surface. Andi had dealt with it, but that didn't mean the idea of something similar happening again didn't stab her occasionally.

Riley gave her the everything's-fine smile that always made Andi melt into safety. "Of course he's fine. I just saddled him."

Andi let out a breath and sat down on a kitchen chair. "Don't scare me like that."

Riley looked Andi up and down. His laughter bubbled over like a spring creek. "I think you're practicing too hard to be the perfect housewife. Why don't we play hooky from the kitchen and ranch chores and go for a ride?"

Andi's heart swelled. *Yes, anywhere!* Her gaze swept the table, the sink full of dishes, and the flour all over the floor.

"Where?" She would clean Mother's kitchen later.

Riley suddenly looked uncomfortable. "Remember that time a couple of years ago when I finally talked you into riding Shasta?"

Andi nodded, not exactly sure where this was going.

"I told you we were going to ride to a special spot of mine. But things kind of got out of hand when you galloped away, and we ended up . . ." His voice trailed away.

Oh, yes. Andi remembered it very well. "That imaginary hideaway you told me about." She didn't believe him then, and she wasn't sure she could believe him now.

She cringed. *I should believe him.*

Riley was nothing but kindness all the time. But he was also firm and liked to remind Andi that she didn't know everything. He confirmed it right then. "Yes, my princess. The one you insisted I made up just to trick you into going for a ride."

Heat crept into Andi's cheeks at the memory. Once she'd resolved that horrible time and forgiven everybody, she should have realized Riley would never lie to her—or purposely trick her.

I was out of my head during those terrible two months to think anything else.

But for some reason, neither Andi nor Riley had brought up his hideaway again. Until today.

"Do you mean . . ." She leaped out of her seat.

"I think today is the perfect day to finally show you that hideaway of mine." He lifted a finger and wagged it in Andi's flour-dusted face. "Contrary to what you told me, I know you've never been there before. If you had, you would remember it."

Andi scowled. She still found it hard to believe she didn't know every square acre of the Circle C ranch and beyond. A new thought came to her. "Is this secret hideaway on the Circle C or on what will soon become our own Memory Creek ranch?"

That caught Riley off guard. He pondered a bit then shrugged. "You know what? I'm not sure."

Then he chuckled. "Does it matter? It's mine for no other reason than nobody else will ever find it. Chad's a family man now, what with a new wife and all. Plus, running this spread takes all his time. He's grown up way past hunting around for secret spots."

Andi grinned. So long as Riley or she never spilled the beans, they could claim any secret hideaway as their own.

Prickles of pure joy and excitement skittered up Andi's spine at the idea of this outing. In a burst of love, she threw her arms around Riley's neck and kissed his cheek.

"Gee-whiz, Andi," Riley said, grinning. "I'll have to come up with more surprises. The reward is worth it." He rubbed his cheek. "So long as I can pass on the floury extras."

Andi playfully swatted his arm. "When can we leave?" She couldn't wait to get out of this kitchen.

"Change into riding clothes," Riley said. "Since you're still under your family, you'd better check with your Mother, out of courtesy. Then pack a lunch." He furrowed his brow. "It's quite a distance, if I remember right."

Andi grinned. She knew he remembered just fine.

Chapter 2

A ndi couldn't remember being more excited about anything than finding a secret hideaway today. Sure, there were other things that had sent her flying high above the clouds—when Chad first gave Andi her special spot, the spot where Riley and her brothers were building the soon-to-be-wed couples' new home.

Seeing baby Taffy was also memorable.

Those were little-girl excitements. Thinking she'd found gold with Cory one spring when she was nine was the most exciting thing Andi had ever experienced.

I'm grown up now, Andi thought while she changed clothes and asked Mother if she could escape for a couple of hours. She was sure other high adventures awaited her

Like holding my own little baby. That would outshine any gold nugget. But for now, finding Riley's special spot was high on her list of exciting adventures.

Besides, the idea that he knew a spot on the ranch that she knew nothing about didn't sit well with Andi. She needed Riley to prove it. This precious spot might lie beyond the borders of the ranch.

Then I would be right.

Somehow, though, she doubted Riley was confused by the Circle C ranch borders.

Andi flew through packing their lunch. She tied the bundle to Shasta's saddle horn and climbed aboard.

For a wonder, Riley told Tucker to stay home. That was a first. Riley's small, loyal collie was always at his heels.

Andi didn't question it, although Tucker looked mighty forlorn lying on the porch with his head on his paws.

Poor, lonely thing.

"We'll be back soon," she promised the dog, but he didn't even wag his tail at her words.

Andi and Riley rode for a long, long time. For most of the way she recognized markers.

A tree zapped by lightning and now blackened and dead.

A rocky outcropping in the shape of a giant ants' nest.

The huge log lying over a seasonal creek.

Andi knew these landmarks well and told Riley so. She couldn't help smirking to herself.

Riley just smiled and kept Dakota at a steady lope. Andi nudged Shasta to keep up.

Pretty soon Riley pulled Dakota to a stop and pointed toward the northeast. "See that row of striated rocks a few miles away?"

"Those are the Banded Rocks," Andi said. "I always wanted to see what was on the other side, but there's no way through them. You have to ride all the way around them. Cory and I tried it once, a long time ago."

Riley's lips twitched. "What happened?"

Andi rolled her eyes. "There's nothing beyond that row of towering rock formations but more foothills. Dull ones."

She sighed her disappointment. She'd been here before. There was nothing new to explore. Nothing that she hadn't already explored, right down to the smallest pebble.

Riley didn't say anything. Instead, he nudged Dakota into a faster lope and headed straight for the Banded Rocks.

Andi followed along on Shasta, but some of the sunshine had gone out of this adventure. Even the possibility of "I told you so" didn't make her feel happy. She'd looked forward to a truly secret place she'd never explored.

They finally pulled up near a row of rocks standing like a tall, broken fence.

Andi looked up. *Yep, the same rocks.* They had probably stood like this since Noah's flood.

Riley dismounted.

Andi wrinkled her eyebrows. There was no shade here, and no trees. Good thing they'd watered the horses a short time ago. "Where are you going?"

"You'll see. Follow me."

Puzzled, Andi slid off Shasta. She grabbed his reins and urged him along.

Instead of taking an old animal trail that circled around to the back—a fair distance and one Andi was not looking forward to, especially since she knew what lay on the other side—Riley headed straight for a narrow gap between two of the enormous, striped boulders.

He passed by the gap and ducked behind a third boulder.

"Where in the world are you going?" Andi demanded. "This trail goes nowhere. Cory and I once spent a full day poking our noses into and around the piles and piles of rocks, to no satisfying end."

Riley didn't reply. He smiled and motioned her to follow.

A minute later, she and Riley were staring at a solid rock cliff. "Riley, I told you so. These trails lead—"

"Oh, ye of little faith." Riley chuckled and tied Dakota to the half-dead branch of a scrawny pine tree. It appeared to be growing straight out of the boulder.

It wasn't really. The tree grew between the cracks, but there was barely enough dirt to hold its meager roots in place.

"Tie Shasta and come along, my doubting Thomasina."

Andi laughed at the way he'd turned "Doubting Thomas" into a girl's name. She did what he said.

Riley grasped Andi's hand and led her past the horses. He took a sharp left that clearly led to another dead end.

Then, just before they bumped into a high rock face, Riley turned right.

By now, Andi was hanging onto his hand for life. This had suddenly turned into a rock maze, a labyrinth suited for the Minotaur of the old Greek myths.

Where is my ball of string when I need it? For the first time since beginning this adventure, Andi had an inkling that perhaps Riley was telling the truth.

For sure, she had never explored the innards of this rock jungle. She would not have been doing so now if Riley wasn't giving her hand a tug every few minutes.

It was cool as an autumn evening in the shadow of the Banded Rocks. Scattered droppings along the way told Andi that rodents and other small creatures claimed this place, but chances were good that nobody but Riley had entered here since the creation of the world.

Andi shivered. It was eerie, and so quiet.

Riley let go of Andi's hand just then and dropped to all fours. "It's a tight squeeze," he said, "but it's not far."

He vanished into a narrow, rocky tunnel.

Andi's breath caught. She did not want to follow him through that narrow opening. But neither did she want to be left behind with shadows and animal scat.

Andi went down on her hands and knees and gingerly followed her brave leader through the narrow opening through the rocks. Her breath came in little gasps.

I don't like tight, enclosed spaces. Now I know why!

It wasn't dark. As soon as Riley passed through, light poured into Andi's face. She blinked and kept crawling. A dozen paces later, her head poked through. Riley reached out and helped her stand up. She gasped.

Chapter 3

Andi was not prepared for what greeted her. Several yards away, a gushing spring bubbled up from under the rocks. It flowed swiftly toward a glade that seemed surreal.

The California foothills were anything but lush, especially during the late summer and autumn. Spring poppies and bright-green grass quickly turned golden by May. It was called the Golden State for a reason.

Only at the higher elevations, where the source of water was not completely depleted, could trees grow tall and green, and the undergrowth stay lush so late in the season.

It couldn't happen here. Not in this desolate area near the Banded Rocks. Not unless it rained and rained. Which it hadn't. Not since the end of April.

This glade didn't seem to notice the lack of summer rain.

The water emptied into a small pond surrounded by a thick clover carpet. Wildflowers Andi had not seen since last spring grew in bunches near the pond. Aspens and poplars grew thickly.

Andi heard *ribbit, ribbit,* and the sound caught her off guard. Frogs? In September? Birds of all kinds—probably the only creatures who could easily access this place—flew back and forth. Swallows snapped up insects mid-air. The birds looked plump and well fed.

Andi stood speechless with wonder. It suddenly didn't matter if Riley had been right and she was wrong. This place was indeed a secret hideaway. Her eyes couldn't drink in the beauty fast enough.

She looked around to get her bearings. The entire glade was surrounded by tall rock "guards."

Just above the eastern edge of the rock cliffs, the Sierra peaks stuck out.

"I know why Cory and I never found this place," Andi murmured. "We went around the entire rock formation."

She pointed. "I'm pretty sure we stood just on the other side of that eastern formation." She shook her head. "We never knew what lay so close . . . but completely impossible to get to."

Riley nodded. "Until I found it."

Andi nodded, speechless.

Riley turned a full circle and smiled at Andi. "Well, what do you think?"

Andi looked up into his smiling face. "Oh, Riley! I never dreamed of anything like this. How did you ever find it?"

He pushed back his hat. "I was after a pesky coyote—"

Andi scowled. *Coyotes! Ugh!*

"Yeah, I'm afraid this hideaway is not perfect. Anyway, I followed the coyote into the rocks, and lo and behold, the animal ducked through the tunnel. I followed it, and when I came out . . ."

He paused and waved his arm. "I saw this. Oh, and I got the coyote by the way." He took Andi's hand. "Come on."

This time, Andi followed gladly. They made their way along the bubbling creek and stopped at the edge of the pond. When Andi sat down, the grass felt like velvet. She crawled to the edge of the water.

For a wonder, the pond was clear as glass. The Banded Rocks reflected back picture-perfect.

The sun wouldn't be around for long, though. The glade wasn't very large. Too soon the sun would slip behind the western cliffs, and this special hideaway would be cast into shadows.

By the looks of it, they had less than an hour to enjoy the beauty of this place. No fish lived in the pond, but plenty of other critters did—water bugs, dragonflies, frogs.

Riley laid a quieting hand on Andi's shoulder and pointed. A rabbit doe with a litter of late-season bunnies hopped into the clover and began munching.

Andi sat still. The little ones scampered and chased each other, but the mama rabbit looked nervous. Every few seconds she sat high on her haunches and looked around.

"I'm pretty sure she scents us," Andi whispered.

Riley put a finger to his lips and nodded.

Andi had been watching the rabbit family for maybe ten minutes, when a large shadow suddenly appeared overhead. She knew what it was, and so did the rabbits.

A hawk swooped low, and the bunnies scattered.

Andi held her breath. *Please, not the bunnies!*

It was a silly thought. Hawks had to eat and feed their babies too, but Andi couldn't help letting out a sigh of relief when the hawk's intended targets ducked into a clump of bushes.

The predator missed them by a whisker.

The rest of the time in the glade passed in such a way that Andi was sure she would always keep this adventure high on her best-ever list. Riley and she talked and talked and talked.

She couldn't remember everything they talked about. There was something about this secret hideaway that made them both feel lazy and restful. Maybe it was the sound of trickling water, or perhaps the smell of something fresh and green and wet in the middle of a dry California autumn.

Whatever it was, Andi didn't want to leave.

Too late she remembered their lunch. She'd left it tied to Shasta's saddle horn.

"Oh, well," Riley said. "We'll remember it next time."

Next time! That sounded nice.

"We'd best get back," Riley said when the rock cliffs cut off the sunshine. He sounded reluctant to go. "The horses have not had such a nice time as we have."

Shasta and Dakota were tied to an old scrub pine in the middle of a rock pile. But they would be fine. It was cool and shady there, and they'd been watered not long before Andi and Riley had reached the Banded Rocks.

They retraced their steps through the tunnel, crisscrossed a number of turns in the rock maze, and finally stumbled outside to the sound of welcoming whinnies. Andi tried to memorize the route.

Riley clearly knew what she was thinking. "Listen, Andi. I want your promise not to come here on your own."

Andi furrowed her brow. Just then, sweet Riley sounded like bossy Chad. This place wasn't dangerous, so why—

"Mostly, I want this to be our special spot," he explained. "The other spot was yours alone, and you shared it. Our new life together will begin there. This glade was my secret spot, but I'm sharing it with you."

When Riley put it that way, Andi was in total agreement. Yes, this was their special spot. Someday, she and Riley would bring their own children here, and wouldn't they all have a marvelous time!

In her mind's eye, Andi saw four or five giggling children, one shouting from Riley's shoulders. They were building camps and scattering the wildlife from one end of the glade to the other with their noise.

She imagined everyone on a far-off Sunday afternoon, eating sandwiches, drinking lemonade, and munching on cookies.

Riley and she would be resting on the blanket, keeping watch so the baby didn't toddle into the pond.

Andi's heart swelled in expectation. *I can't wait . . .*

Peaches, Peaches Everywhere

Circle C Ranch, California, Fall 1885

Mother is determined to make sure I am not lacking in all the housewife skills that Melinda comes by naturally. This, unfortunately, includes putting up peaches.

Andi Carter loved peaches, but she didn't much care for harvesting them. That adventure had backfired five years ago, when big brother Chad caught her in the orchards.

Andi didn't like sitting still to slip the skins from the peaches, either. But it was fast. Much faster than peeling apples. The best part was as soon as the whole slipping skins business was finished, she'd always been allowed to run and play, or to go riding with Taffy.

Not today.

When she entered the kitchen, she nearly tripped over half a dozen heaping bushel baskets of peaches. They rested side by side in a row pushed up against the kitchen wall.

The back door banged open, and Chad hauled in another basket. Riley followed with one more.

"What are you doing?" Andi asked.

Chad pushed his hat back and grinned. "Mother is canning peaches today, and so are you."

Andi shook her head. "Uh-uh. You told me there's about ten miles of fences to—"

"Your mother wants you to learn the whole process of putting up peaches," Riley chimed in. "I think it's a swell idea. I love peach cobbler, peach pie, peach—"

"Hold on!" Andi raised a hand to stop Riley's chatter. "I already know how to can peaches."

Mother glided into the kitchen just then. "You know how to slip the skins from the peaches," she said. "It's unlikely you know what comes after that." She smiled.

Andi's mind drew a blank. There was something about sugar and hot water and clean jars. She gulped. Mother was right.

"It's high time you learned to preserve peaches using a water bath and jars. Nila and Luisa have been up since the crack of dawn washing jars, rings, and lids."

Mother left no room for an argument. She secured Riley's help dragging the first basket of round, fuzzy balls nearer to the table.

Andi snagged a peach as he went by. She took a bite. *Delicious!*

Riley winked at her. "You have fun now. I'm off to check those fences. Then Chad needs my help on a new corral project."

"Wanna trade?" Andi whispered. Stretching barbed wire sounded likes heaps of fun compared to boiling water in a hot kitchen on what promised to be a scorching day.

He chuckled. "Not for all the gold in California."

Mother handed Andi a spare apron, rolled up her sleeves, and said, "Let's get started."

Just then Chad's new wife, Ellie, entered the kitchen. "Could you use some help?"

Andi opened her mouth to offer Ellie her place, but Mother gave her *the look*. "That would be wonderful, Ellianna."

"You can watch me, Andi," Ellie offered. "Believe it or not, I've canned peaches before. My Aunt Rose taught me years and years ago."

Andi gave Ellie a weak smile. *I should know how to can by now too.*

For all the stories of how she'd been a rough and tumble girl in a broken-down gold camp, Ellie was miles ahead of Andi in the housekeeping area.

Determined to learn this peach preserving as fast as she could, Andi donned the apron Mother had handed her and set to work. The faster she accepted this task, the sooner the day would end.

Ellie grabbed another apron and began sorting peaches for the first round of blanching. "We'll dip the fruit in boiling water. That makes their skins slip off slick as anything."

Andi nodded. She knew this.

Mother took over and gave orders faster than Chad. Mix up the sugar-water recipe. Dip the peaches. Plunge them in cold water. Cut them in half. Pit them. Slip the skins.

This part was easy! Andi's years and years of slipping skins made her faster even than Ellie. Every so often, an entire peach half disappeared into Andi's mouth. The sweet juiciness dripped down her chin.

The morning raced by. Andi's excitement grew. Why, she liked canning peaches! She liked it much better than making applesauce.

How easy is this? she thought.

Skin the peach, slice it in half, and put the halves in the jar. Pour in the syrup and put on the rubber sealing ring.

Next, seal the jar and lower it into the huge water-bath canner. Boil half an hour and . . . done!

When Mother removed the first seven jars of golden-yellow peaches, Andi grinned. "They're so pretty!"

"I plan to let you set aside a few dozen jars for after you're married and in your own home," Mother said, smiling. "After all, you're helping with the entire process today."

"Oh, thank you, Mother!"

By early afternoon, Andi was actually enjoying herself. Mother and Ellie took time to slice some bread and pour a cup of coffee for lunch, but Andi was not hungry. Too many peaches.

It was fun to work with Mother and Andi's new sister-in-law, laughing and telling stories. Maybe even more fun than stretching barbed wire.

Too bad Melinda hadn't joined them, or Lucy.

Andi considered. No, Justin's wife would not feel much like joining this peach party. Not in this heat. She was only two months away from giving birth to their second baby.

Mother wanted to make sure Andi learned every step of the canning process. "Boiling the jars is the most important step, sweetheart," she said, brushing aside a sweaty lock of hair.

Probably the hottest and most miserable part too, Andi figured.

"Make sure the water is boiling before you count the time," Mother warned. "if you aren't careful, every jar of peaches will spoil. All our hard work for nothing."

"Sure, Mother." Andi didn't intend to let all their work go to waste. She would keep an eye on the clock and give the peaches a full, rolling bath.

Yes sirree!

That would be the easiest part of the entire process.

***

Andi was feeling mighty proud of herself. She couldn't wait to show Riley her beautiful work. She'd skinned those peaches herself. She'd cut them. She'd packed them in the jars. She could see Riley's mouth-watering grin already!

"Andrea."

Mother's voice pulled Andi from her daydreaming. She handed her daughter the long-handled, pincer-like jar lifter. "You watched me take the first seven jars out of the canner. Now, you do the same."

She indicated seven jars ready for processing. "Lift these jars into the canner the same way I took the others out."

Andi nodded. This looked easy as pie.

"Make sure you keep that water boiling good and hard," Mother instructed. "It can't cool down. And keep a finger-length of water above the tops of the jars."

Then she turned aside and left Andi to her task.

The simmering water was smooth as glass. Little tendrils of steam rose. It wasn't boiling, so Andi took Mother's words to heart. She stoked up the cook stove and got the fire hotter.

It wasn't but a few minutes until the water began to turn over in a nice, rolling boil. Perfect! No peaches would go bad under Andi's watch. *No sirree!*

Pleased as punch with herself, she latched on to the first jar and lifted it high. She lowered it into the water as quickly as she could in order to get them all boiling at the same time.

Pop. It was a quiet sound, one Andi nearly missed. She furrowed her brow. *Hmm? What was that?*

She peered at the jar. It looked fine.

Soon, seven lovely jars of peaches were boiling away. Andi put the large lid on top of the canner and checked the time. While the peaches boiled, Andi went back to filling jars and eating peaches.

"Canning peaches is not that hard," she told Mother. "So far, I haven't made one mistake. Won't Riley be proud of me?"

Mother agreed. So did Ellie.

Andi kept the fire stoked. She barely noticed the sweat dripping down the back of her neck. Seven jars of processed peaches stood in a row on the counter like proud soldiers. Seven more would soon join them.

When exactly thirty minutes had passed, Andi grabbed the jar lifter and took off the canner lid. The water was boiling along.

She settled the lifter on the first jar and lifted it.

The jar came up with the lifter, but the peaches did not. They drained out of the jar and plopped back into the boiling water, where they tumbled around and around. Some peaches floated near the top.

Andi gaped at the jar hanging by the lifter. It was empty. Worse, it was missing its bottom. *What in the world?*

Andi was so shocked she just stood there staring at the empty jar. The bottom of that jar had vanished.

She set the broken jar aside and went after the next full one in the canner.

Splash! Andi was left holding another empty jar. More peaches joined the others swimming around in the canner.

She caught her breath. This couldn't be happening!

Andi glanced at the row of cooling peaches. The bottoms had not fallen out of Mother's jars.

She looked back into the canner. The five remaining jars stood up straight. They looked perfect.

Andi did not feel very confident now, but the jars must come out. She pinched the top of another jar, squeezed her eyes shut, and carefully lifted it from the water.

At last! The jar looked fine.

Andi let out a sigh of relief and carried it over to the counter. Then she fished around for the next jar. It too came up with the lifter.

Then *splash, splash, splash,* the last three jars came up empty.

Unbelievable!

Andi peeked behind her shoulder. So far, Mother and Ellie had not seen this little drama playing out. They were peeling and pitting peaches, chatting away.

"M-mother," Andi stammered, holding up a broken jar.

Mother turned around. Ellie turned too. She clapped a hand over her mouth.

"My goodness!" Mother exclaimed and hurried over. "How many jars—"

She broke off when she saw two full jars of peaches and five empty, bottomless jars. "Andrea!" Her breath came out in a whoosh.

"Oh, Mother, what did I do wrong?" Andi was close to tears. This was so humiliating.

Ellie joined Mother and Andi at the cook stove. The water continued to bubble merrily. The peaches rolled and floated in the boiling water.

All those peaches. Five full jars. Andi slumped, defeated. What a waste!

Mother wrinkled her forehead. "Did you put the jars into the simmering water before you stoked the fire?"

Andi shook her head. "You told me to make sure the water was boiling good and hard. I got it boiling then put the jars in."

"Oh, dear," Mother said in a quiet voice. "I'm sorry, Andrea. I thought you knew not to put a glass jar into boiling water."

No, Andi didn't know that. But she did know how to lasso a stubborn calf. She could even help during a troubled foaling.

Did that count? Probably not.

"The water needs to heat up slowly," Mother explained.

Andi looked at her mother blankly.

"The cold glass jars expand too quickly when they hit the hot water and . . ." She left the rest unsaid.

And pop! Andi filled in mentally. *Well, live and learn.* She would never make this mistake again. The strangest thing was that the jars hadn't broken on impact. Those sneaky things had quietly popped out their bottoms but held together until it was time to take them out.

Just waiting to spring a horrible surprise on her.

Oooh! It would have been a thousand times better to see the first jar break when it touched the roiling water. Andi would have at least been on her guard.

This disaster put them behind. Mother and Andi fished out the boiling peaches. "It's not a total waste, sweetheart," she tried to comfort her daughter. "We'll rinse the peaches well to make sure no glass particles are stuck to them, and then we can make a lovely peach cobbler for supper."

Andi nodded, but peach cobbler didn't sound very good right then.

The huge enamel water bath canner had to be dumped out and refilled with water. Then began the long, *long* wait to bring the water up to simmering for the next bath.

It took about an hour. In the late-afternoon heat. Ellie rinsed the peaches, and Andi recovered the five jar bottoms. It was the most peculiar thing. Each bottom fit perfectly onto its matching jar. No cracks. No splinters.

Andi shook her head. Those traitorous jars!

No, this was my own fault.

The next time Andi looked at the clock it was six o'clock. She was dead tired. And still not hungry.

Riley and Chad came home to a kitchen overflowing with sticky counters, a sticky table, peach peelings, crocks of peach pits, and four dozen jars of peaches.

And the peach cobbler Mother had whipped up.

Our supper.

THREE

TEMPORARY TEACHER

SAN JOAQUIN VALLEY, CALIFORNIA, LATE FALL 1885

I figured I'd dodged a bullet when Ellie Coulter stepped in to replace old Miss Hall. Melinda and Mother had pegged me for that teaching position, but thankfully I got out of it. Or at least I thought I did.

Chapter 1

Andrea Carter stood firm whenever her mother or sister brought up the Fresno Grammar School teaching position. *I despised school as a student.* How could she ever lug an armful of books and sit around listening to children recite their ABCs?

She shivered in remembered horror.

Ellie had quite literally saved Andi's sanity. Even after her engagement to Chad, her soon-to-be-sister kept on teaching. She loved her students, even the ornery ones.

Andi felt a tickle of uncertainty when Ellie and Chad "tied the knot" in September. Would the school board allow Ellie to keep teaching? Married women just didn't do that sort of thing.

"But you never pay any attention to what others think, right, Chad?" Andi asked at supper the day the newlyweds returned home from their honeymoon trip to New York City.

"What are you talking about?" Chad asked.

Andi shrugged. "Ellie's still going to teach, right?" Her heart fluttered. *Please say yes!*

Chad pointed his fork at Justin, who was enjoying a rare night around the Circle C table. "It's not my call. Or Ellie's. It's the school board's. Ask big brother." He promptly went back to eating.

"No worries, Andi." Justin chuckled. "We found a teacher to take Ellie's place."

Andi darted a quick glance at her new sister-in-law. Would Ellie be disappointed?

Ellie's face lit up. "Who, Justin?"

It appeared Ellie was happy to settle down and be a rancher's wife. *Good. Maybe she'll want to go riding this afternoon.*

"Virginia Foster."

Andi nearly choked on her water. "Virginia?"

It figured. Virginia had always been the smartest scholar. Always at the top of her class in every subject.

Mr. Foster had often boasted of his daughter's tutoring skills, and Andi assumed Virginia went along with it to avoid going against her father.

But no. During their last year of school together, before Andi had that dreadful accident on Taffy, Virginia spent more classroom time helping other students than she did studying on her own.

She'd even gone to school an extra year!

Andi put down her glass. Yes, it made sense that Virginia would slide into a teacher's position when she was old enough. *I'm glad! Better Virginia than me.*

Andi's life was close to perfect. She spent most of her days outdoors. When work was over, she and Riley went riding—

and planning their new life together.

***

Only six months before I become Mrs. Andrea Prescott!

The month of January came in with dense valley fog and rain. And more rain.

"Andrea, how would you like a job in town?" Mother asked at Sunday dinner during one especially stormy afternoon.

Andi's fork stopped halfway to her mouth. "Job?" She wrinkled her forehead. She already had a job. She helped Chad run the ranch. "What kind of job?" she asked suspiciously.

As usual, the entire Carter family had gathered. Sunday dinner together had become a tradition, one Andi would never tire of. It was especially nice that Riley was included, now that they were officially engaged to be married.

Except, sometimes Mother used the occasion to corral Andi into doing something she didn't want to do. It was much harder to say no in front of the entire family—plus Riley—than it was to say no over a quick breakfast before heading out to lasso a horse or steer.

Mother frowned. "Haven't you heard? Virginia Foster has succumbed to fever and chills. Dr. Weaver thinks she might have influenza."

Andi swallowed her forkful of potatoes and nodded. "I heard. I figured they'd get somebody to take her place."

She glanced at Ellie, who was seated across the table. "I'd have thought you would jump at the chance to get back into the classroom. Surely, the school board would make an exception for a temporary teacher."

Ellie shook her head. "I offered my services, but the school board turned me down." She gave Justin an accusing look.

"They prefer not to set a precedent of having a married woman teaching in the classroom."

Andi couldn't figure out the sense in that. "Why, Mother taught our class when I was small. Miss Hall sprained her ankle, and Mother took over for several weeks." She scowled at Justin.

He held up his hands in defense. "Ladies, please! The board will consider Ellie as a last resort, but first they want to explore other options." He looked at Andi and smiled.

Oh, no, you don't! Andi immediately put up her guard.

"Justin thinks it would be a wonderful idea if you took over for Virginia," Mother said. "This winter is especially cold and rainy. Chad says you can have a month or two off."

Now Andi scowled at Chad. "Thanks for that, big brother." She was not thankful at all.

Mother smiled. "Think how much nicer it would be to spend the day inside a warm classroom rather than on horseback in the rain and chill."

"I agree," Melinda chirped.

Andi swallowed. *I'm outnumbered.*

When Mother, big brother, and big sister all agreed, the baby of the family had no chance to wriggle away. Though, she couldn't help thinking about that lousy fence project she'd volunteered for.

In the rain.

Still . . . rain? Classroom? Rain? Class—

Nope. Rain won.

"What about Riley?" Andi grasped at straws. She gave Riley a pleading look. *Say something!*

Riley said something, all right. "Don't worry about me, Andi. I'll miss your sunny smile, but I'll be fine for a month or so."

"You'll have time in the evenings and on weekends to spend time with your fiancé." Mother brightened. It looked like she was going to win this round.

"Riley can drive you to town and pick you up."

She sent a meaningful glance at Chad, who nodded. "I reckon I could let him off for a couple of hours every day."

Andi was perfectly capable of hitching up the buggy and driving herself to and from town, but she kept quiet. If she ended up teaching, she'd at least get an hour every morning and every afternoon to be with Riley.

Besides, it was no fun hitching up a buggy in the rain.

But . . . "You know I can't stand being trapped all day in a classroom," Andi argued. "I thought I was done with those days when I graduated. Chad told me I could help run the ranch. That's what I'm good at. Not teaching."

Mother's face fell. "You're too old to be told what to do, sweetheart. You are almost a married woman. However, you are not yet married. Even Justin thinks you would be perfect for this position."

She reached over and patted Andi's chilly hand. "It's only for eight short weeks. The term will be over then. Hopefully Virginia will be able to begin the new term."

Andi slumped. It might take longer than eight weeks for pale, skinny Virginia to regain her strength, especially after something as serious as influenza.

She took a deep breath and looked at Ellie and Chad.

Chad flashed Andi a sympathetic look, and Ellie smiled. *You might as well give in, little sister,* their eyes told her.

Andi looked at Mother. "All right. I'll do it."

It's only for eight weeks.

Mother smiled at Justin.

He chuckled. "Very nice, Mother. You were right."

Andi frowned at Justin. "Right about what?"

"Mother told me to leave this to her." He shrugged. "And it worked. I'll ride into town and let the school board know."

Andi nodded glumly.

By the way, you were our first choice." He winked at her. "You'll start tomorrow, all right?"

"I reckon." Andi sighed. "Might as well get it over with."

She'd been run over. No doubt about it. Not with a train engine, but with that Carter sense of responsibility.

And with her desire to please her mother.

Andi could have told Justin "no" without a glimmer of conscience. If Chad had asked, she'd have laughed out loud. Even Melinda couldn't have talked her into this.

But Mother? It was harder to say no when this was obviously something Mother cared a great deal about.

"You'll enjoy teaching," Ellie spoke up. "The children are sweet." She laughed. "Most of them, anyway. It's rewarding to see their eyes light up when they understand a problem. The term will fly by. You'll see."

"One can only hope," Andi muttered, reaching for her glass.

She glanced at Mother. Her face was radiant.

She wants this for me. For her sake, I won't complain. Andi swallowed the rest of her water in one gulp. *I will act happy.*

Even though she dreaded this job more than she had dreaded anything in her life.

Chapter 2

Sunday evening dragged. Andi reluctantly folded her split skirts and put them away. Her stained, rumpled blouses joined the skirts. She rummaged through her wardrobe and drew out a new, white shirtwaist.

An old-lady blouse, she thought with a sigh.

High collar, a line of pearl buttons. Tiny pleats running up and down each side of the buttons. And those puffed sleeves at the shoulders? *Oh, well.*

She laid the shirtwaist next to a Tartan-plaid skirt. It was the longest and fullest skirt she owned. Her split-skirt hung halfway to her ankles. This skirt brushed the ground. After all, grown-up young ladies didn't let their ankles show.

At least not on purpose.

Andi went to bed with too many worries on her mind. She tossed and turned all night. Her head pounded.

Her headache did not improve when she piled her long, thick braid on top of her head the next morning. Heaven forbid that it should fall down her back and dangle loosely for every gossipy old lady in Fresno to gawk at and wag her tongue in shock.

Andi struggled with the button hook until her high-topped, high-heeled shoes were snuggly in place over thick black stockings.

She glanced in the looking glass before leaving her room. "Don't trip down the stairs," she mumbled to her reflection. "For sure don't slide down the bannister."

She grabbed a stack of school books and headed downstairs for breakfast. Her appetite fled.

Chad's eyebrows shot up. "Well, don't you look—"

"Not a word, Chad," Andi snapped. "I mean it."

He closed his mouth. But he held a napkin to his lips, for sure hiding a grin. His eyes twinkled.

Andi glared at him and reached for the syrup pitcher.

"Better hurry and eat, Andrea," Mother went on. "You don't want to be late. Not on your first day."

Andi muttered, "Yes, ma'am," and poured maple syrup over her hotcakes. Then she stabbed at the sweet, sticky mess.

Her stomach felt twisted in a dozen knots. *I can't do this. Teaching has never been for me. What if I fail?*

She pushed the plate away. "I'm not hungry."

Mother gave Andi an encouraging smile. "You needn't be nervous. You'll do splendidly."

"Yeah, little sister," Chad chimed in. "You're a Carter. You can do anything you set your mind to."

"Yes, but *teaching*?" Andi clenched her fork until her knuckles turned white. "I'd rather work cattle any day."

Mother laughed. "You'll do fine, sweetheart. Trust me."

"I think so too." Ellie winked.

Andi scowled and scratched at her leg. *These bothersome stockings!* "I hope you're right. May I be excused?"

"At least eat a little breakfast," Mother urged. "You'll be hungry come lunch time."

Andi wasn't sure about that, but she choked down a few bites. Then she wiped her face, rose, and kissed her mother good-bye. "I'll see you this afternoon."

"Don't forget your books, and the lunch Luisa prepared."

Andi headed for the kitchen on the run, which wasn't easy to do in heels. She grabbed the tin lunch pail and bolted outside.

Riley stood next to the buggy. "Good morning, Teacher," he greeted her with a wide grin. "Ready for your first day?" He held out a hand to help her into the buggy.

"Not a chance." Andi accepted his help and swung into the rig. Her voice fell. "Don't tell Mother or Chad, but I'm scared silly. Look." She held out her shaking hands.

"Hmm." Riley swung up beside her and chirruped to the horse. "It can't be all that bad. I think you'll do swell."

Andi fidgeted with her skirt. "I wish I could stay here and help you mend fences this afternoon."

Riley didn't reply.

"Even catching a chill from this damp weather sounds better than sitting in a stifling classroom all day," she said.

"I see your mother has you all slicked up." Riley chuckled. "I hardly recognized such a beautiful young lady."

"*Riley!*" Andi slouched in the seat. "No more, please." She shook her head. "I wish Mother was taking over this job, not me. I don't know the first thing about teaching."

She chewed on her lip. "I'm only seventeen. Some of those eleven-year-old boys are bigger than I am."

This last part came out in a whisper.

"The Campbell boy is no Johnny Wilson." Riley reached over and squeezed her hand. "Besides, every kid in the lower grades knows who you are. They know you have three big brothers. Nobody will misbehave. Relax. You'll do fine."

It did no good to argue. Riley always found the good in any situation. "Just hear what Chad has planned for me today."

Andi broke into a small smile. *Good ol' Riley!* Her spirits rose. "What?"

Riley kept Andi's mind off the quickly approaching school day. He filled her ears with ranch talk and jokes. By the time they reached town, Andi felt much better.

"Well, here we are, Teacher." Riley drew the buggy up beside the school and offered Andi his hand to climb down. "Watch the wheel," he warned. "See you this afternoon."

Andi looked up into her fiancé's cheerful hazel eyes. With all her heart she wished Riley could stay. Instead of begging, she said, "I hope you're praying for me. I'm going to need it."

"Sure thing." He gave her an encouraging smile. "You can do all things through Him, Andi. God is with you."

Andi smiled back. "Thanks." There was no one in the whole world like Riley. "I'll see you later."

Andi turned and mounted the porch steps. She looked over her shoulder just in time to see Riley waving as he drove the buggy away from the schoolyard and out of town.

Riley is right. I can do this . . . with God's help. Please, God, help me. I know I can't do it alone.

A flow of confidence and peace surged through her. With a smile and a light heart, Andi entered the schoolroom.

Chapter 3

Hands shaking, Andi hung up her wraps and set her lunch pail and books on the teacher's desk. *My desk*, she corrected herself.

She'd expected the room to be dank and chilly. Instead, a warm glow radiated from the potbellied stove in the corner. Which kind student had come early to light the fire?

"Miss Carter?"

Andi whirled from warming her hands. Mr. Foster stood at the back of the classroom, near the staircase that led up to his own class.

"M-Mr. F-Foster," she stammered. "You startled me."

Andi's former teacher folded his arms across his chest and smiled. "Forgive me. I just wanted to see if you have everything you need."

"I think so."

There was nothing more uncomfortable to Andi than speaking with her strict schoolmaster on equal terms. It disoriented her. For a moment, she was an erring twelve-year-old pupil again, wondering what fault the teacher had found with her this time.

"Did you start the fire?" she asked, breaking the silence.

"Yes, I did," Mr. Foster replied with a nod. "I start a fire every morning for Virginia." He looked worried at the mention of his daughter's name. "I thought you might appreciate it as well."

"I do! Thank you," Andi said. "How is Virginia?"

"Quite ill, but the doctor believes she will recover." He made a *tsk-tsk* noise with his tongue. "Nasty business, this influenza." His mouth turned up in a warm smile. "Virginia appreciates you taking her class and has every confidence in you." He smiled wider. "So have I."

With that, Mr. Foster turned and headed to the entry. "I'd best ring the bell. It is eight fifty-five."

Soon, footsteps clattered up the porch steps, and thirty-five eager young pupils swarmed into the classroom. Even with a new school on the other side of town, this older building was still crowded.

Not one empty seat. So many children!

Andi swallowed the lump that formed in her throat. Her heart was thrumming out of control.

The children chattered and giggled. Books thudded onto desktops. Lids creaked open and then banged shut.

Andi's heels clicked against the wooden floorboards. When she got to the blackboard, she picked up a stick of chalk and turned around to face her students.

Sudden silence. Thirty-five faces—some rubbed clean, some dirty with breakfast crumbs—gaped at her.

Andi flushed. "Good morning, children." She cleared her throat. "I am Miss Carter."

One of the little boys burst into laughter. "We know! And we know Miss Foster's sick in bed." He winked to his seatmate then looked back at his new teacher. "You're Andi."

The others nodded and shuffled their feet.

Andi felt at a sudden disadvantage. They all knew her name. And why not? Two short years ago, she had sat just one floor above these children in this very building. She'd even romped with them occasionally during recess.

This is not starting out well at all. She didn't know the names of even a quarter of her pupils.

She turned around and scribbled her name on the board.

Miss Carter

"You might as well know right off . . . Charley," she said, thankful she knew the little boy with the red hair and freckles. "I'm *Miss Carter* to you." She pointed the chalk at Charley's seatmate. "To you too, Wes."

She faced the rest of the class. Her flutters vanished. "To all of you."

She took a deep breath. "When this is all over and Miss Foster is back, then you can call me Andi again. Well, maybe," she added.

Just what was she these days? A young lady? A ranch hand? An overgrown schoolgirl?

There was no response.

"Children?"

"Yes, Miss Carter."

Andi wracked her brain to remember what Mother told

the children all those years ago when she had taken Miss Hall's place for a few weeks.

Andi couldn't remember, so she made up something. Something she hoped sounded firm yet friendly. "I'm sure that if you give me your very best attention and respect, we'll get along well, don't you think?"

Around the room, heads nodded. "Yes, ma'am."

"Good." She bored an especially mischievous-looking boy in the back row with a stern look. His hand was inside his desk. "What's your name?"

The boy's hand withdrew from his desk as if it was on fire. "Cody."

Andi couldn't help it. She grinned. *Cody* sounded awfully close to *Cory.* "Listen here, Cody. You've got some kind of critter in your desk, don't you?"

His eyes nearly bugged out. "Yes, ma'am, but I—"

Andi waved his words away. "Never mind. I know there's a frog or a spider or maybe a snake in your desk. Keep it there all day, for all I care. There's only one rule. If I see it, it's mine. You understand?"

Cody's round blue eyes turned even wider. "Yes'm."

"Good." Andi motioned the children to stand. "Let's sing 'America' and then I'll find the Bible passage where Miss Foster left off before she became ill."

Thirty-five smiling children leaped to their feet. They sang "America" with more gusto than Andi had ever heard—not in all her years of attending school.

The rest of the day passed quickly. Before Andi knew it, the clock read four o'clock. *Finally! I can go home.*

A scuffling noise at the back of the classroom caught Andi's attention. Hat in hand, Riley stood at the door. He was grinning broadly.

"Is that fella your beau, An—Miss Carter?' Charley asked without raising his hand.

Andi rose and pushed in her chair. She was so happy to see Riley that she didn't care who knew she and Riley were engaged. "No, Charley," she said in a loud, clear voice. "Mr. Prescott is my fiancé."

At that, the entire class turned around and stared.

"Howdy, kids." Riley waved his hat at the crowd. "Did you all behave today?"

"Yes, sir!" thirty-five voices shouted.

Andi dismissed the class, and they raced for the door like a herd of stampeding cattle.

Riley jumped out of the way just in time. He watched the tail end of the crowd vanish out of the schoolhouse then turned to Andi.

She smiled at him. "I made it." A long, grateful breath whooshed from her body. Her muscles relaxed. Surely, nothing could be as bad as the first day of school.

"Looks that way." Riley shut the damper on the stove and helped Andi clean the blackboard.

By the time they climbed into the rig, Andi was ready to collapse. The day hadn't gone too badly, she told Riley. "I had the children's names sorted out before the noon hour. Better yet, I already know everything the children are learning."

"Well, they are the little ones, after all," Riley reminded her. "No geometry required."

"More or less *little*." She remembered looking up into Joey Campbell's brown eyes when he asked for help in arithmetic. But he was a little gentleman, just like Riley had told her. He'd even kept the fire burning in the stove.

Cody kept his creatures hidden in his desk. Nobody put a frog in Andi's desk or glue on her chair.

She checked before sitting down, though, just to be sure.

Just before she dismissed the class for the noon recess, she'd overheard Charley talking to Oliver. "Don't you dare do that to Andi. You do, and I'll get you good. Just see if I don't!"

Whatever Oliver was thinking about doing, Charley had clearly stopped him cold. She let the *Andi* go . . . for now.

Chapter 4

After a good night's sleep, the next day passed even better. *Why, this is not as bad as I expected.* Andi's joy grew. She didn't stop talking to and from town.

Riley smiled, leaned back, and let her talk. He laughed in the right places, said "good for you" when she told him about Cody's secret pets, and shook his head. "Sure wish you'd been *my* teacher when I was a kid."

Andi punched him on the arm and kept talking.

The whole week passed like a whirlwind. One week down. Seven more to go.

The next Monday, school turned upside down.

It happened during the noon recess. The rain had since come to an end. The sun shone down warm and welcoming.

Why, it must be nearly sixty-five degrees! Andi mused.

She sat on the porch steps enjoying one of Nila's famous tamales and watching the children play. She checked the small timepiece pinned to her bodice. *Half an hour more.*

For an instant, she wished she were on Shasta's back, loping through the rangeland, instead of sitting motionless. She finished her lunch, propped her elbows on her knees, and rested her chin in her hands.

Very unladylike. But it was mighty dull sitting here on the steps, watching all the fun. She felt antsy. She supposed she could go inside and correct papers, but—

Not for the first time that noon hour, a thought sneaked into Andi's head. *I wish I could run and play.*

She sighed.

A grown-up young lady with a teacher's position and neat, tidy clothes—not to mention a despised corset—would never do such a thing.

"Miss Carter! Miss Carter!"

Andi's head snapped up.

Eight-year-old Lillian Travis ran up. Her auburn hair flew in wild tangles about her face, but she pushed it away. Her dress and pinafore were streaked with dirt.

"Lillie!" Andi exclaimed. "Are you all right?"

"Sure, Miss Carter. I was just playing with the others." She hopped from one foot to the other. "We wanna play ante-over, but we're one player short." She grabbed Andi's hand. "Please, Miss Carter, could you play with us? *Please?*"

Andi bit her lip. She could maybe turn a jump rope, but to play ante-over? Was Lillie crazy to ask?

"Charley says you'll do it," Lillie said. "He says you're the best ante-over player ever." She scrunched up her forehead. "He should know. He's ten. He 'members when you used to play during noon recess."

Andi cringed. Charley had a good memory. She'd played ante-over that year, then she'd met Aunt Rebecca's train, rumpled and sweaty. Not a good memory.

"Please?" Lillie's auburn eyes pleaded.

"Oh, all right." Andi rose and brushed off her skirt. After all, who would know? Only she and her pupils were here. Mr. Foster was immured in his classroom upstairs.

But what if—

She glanced around the schoolyard. No townsfolk were in sight. It wouldn't hurt to play for a little while. She grabbed Lillie's hand. "Let's go."

Lillie squealed her joy.

It didn't take Andi long to participate full force in the game. Soon, a number of Mr. Foster's older pupils saw the fun and asked to join in.

Andi should have given the game over to them. The players were more than equal now. But—

"Ante-over!" The ball hurtled over the tall building. Those older boys could really throw a ball!

Smiling, Andi chased, dodged, tossed, and caught the ball. Time flew. Suddenly, Andi was no longer Miss Carter. She was Andi, running and playing as she had longed to do since the minute the sun came out.

During a quick break, Andi stopped to catch her breath and look at the timepiece. Ten minutes until the noon hour was over.

It was time to return to proper Miss Carter and look like a teacher when Mr. Foster came out to ring the bell.

But first . . . one more catch.

From the other side of the schoolhouse came another shout of "ante-over!"

One of the oldest boys had clearly thrown the ball. The schoolhouse was tall—two stories, and that ball cleared the roof with room to spare.

Down, down, down it came, headed straight for—

"Lillie!" Andi shrieked. "Head's up!"

No time. The ball was traveling like a cannon shot. Andi leaped for Lillie and shoved her out from under the flying ball. Then she turned to catch it.

Too late. The ball slammed against Andi's head. She stumbled backward, tripped, and sprawled on the ground.

She lay still, with her breath knocked out. Stars danced before her eyes. Her head pounded.

"Oh, Miss Carter!" Lillie threw herself next to Andi and tried to lift her. "Are you all right?"

Andi sat up and groaned. Her snow-white shirtwaist was a dusty brown. So was her skirt. "Oh, no."

The other children gathered around. They touched her and patted her and tried to brush the dust from her clothes.

One of Mr. Foster's students looked shame-faced. "I'm sorry, Miss Carter." It was Toby Wright. "I threw the ball. I got caught up in the game and forgot about the little kids." He lent Andi his hand and helped her to her feet.

"Thank you, Toby. I'm fine." She smiled, but her head kept pounding.

"Miss Carter!"

Andi turned. "Yes, Charley?"

"A rig's pulling up in front of the schoolhouse. It's full of important-looking men." He shaded his eyes. "Who do you s'pose they are? And what do you think they want?"

All the breath left Andi's body. *Oh no, oh no, oh no!*

"It's the school board," she whispered. "Stopping by to see how the new teacher is coming along, I reckon."

She closed her eyes. *They are going to eat me alive!*

When Andi opened her eyes, she looked at her clothes. Then . . . *worse and worse!* Her long, dark braid had come unfastened during the game. It hung sloppily down her back. Escaping tendrils blew across her cheeks.

No time to try and fix it now. The hairpins were no doubt scattered all over the schoolyard. She gulped.

This would certainly be her last day on the job.

Chapter 5

H urry!" Andi called to her young scholars. "Back inside the classroom."

Just then, the bell rang. Mr. Foster shaded his eyes at the carriage then shrugged and returned indoors.

Easy for him, Andi thought. Mr. Foster never cared if the school board showed up. He was always tidy, and his class was always ready to recite.

This was more than Andi could say about her own pupils. She'd planned a spelling bee this afternoon. Most of the kids were lousy spellers. About as lousy as she was.

Andi groaned. *What a dumb idea. To have a spelling bee to show the board how terrible our spelling is.*

She herded her pupils up the steps and into the classroom. There was no time to warn them to be on their best behavior, which is what the board had probably planned.

Holding up her skirt, Andi bounded up the steps behind her charges and bolted through the door. She narrowly missed tripping over a floorboard and fell into her desk, panting.

Runaway tendrils of dark hair stuck to her sweaty face. She tried tucking her shirtwaist into her waistband, but tufts stuck out every which way.

Too late she remembered her wrap. The cloak was hanging on its hook in the coat room. It would cover her rumpled blouse, but it was too warm to wear it.

Wearing a wrap in an eighty-degree classroom would look mighty suspicious.

Andi closed her eyes and sent up a silent prayer. *Please, please, please have the school board members walk up the stairs to Mr. Foster's room.*

No such luck.

The footsteps of five school board members clomped heavily up the porch steps. Less than a minute later, they stood in a row across the back of the room.

To their credit, none of the children made a sound. They didn't turn around. They had clearly caught Andi's panic and looked scared into silence. Lillie's wide eyes were glassy with tears.

Andi looked at Lillie and gave her head a tiny shake. *Don't cry*, she begged the little girl with her eyes. Then she turned back to the five men.

She knew them all. Mr. Evans, Fresno's undertaker. Tall, unsmiling, and critical of anyone under the age of forty. He always complained about the younger generation.

Mr. Wilson, the bank president. Usually friendly, he took his position as school board trustee very seriously. He probably still envisioned Andi as a twelve-year-old.

Judge Morrison looked stern. He'd been a school trustee for more years than Andi could remember. He didn't put up with any monkey business and had given Miss Hall a hard time about four years ago.

A young farmer, Mr. Jason Bartlett, was a new member. With two schools in town, the board had expanded. He looked solemn, as if he wasn't sure what was expected from a trustee.

Then there was Justin. Andi's brother stood at the end of the row. A slight frown wrinkled his forehead. Other than that, he waited with the rest of the group.

Andi swallowed and pasted a smile on her face. Why hadn't Justin warned her the school board was going to pop in on her today? *Traitor!*

When he gave her a sympathetic look, Andi realized Justin had not known about the visit ahead of time. She apologized silently and steadied herself to face the music.

"Good afternoon, Miss Carter," Mr. Evans said in a scratchy voice.

Andi did her best to look like a serious, grown-up teacher. She sat ramrod straight, hands clasped, and wished the floor would swallow her up. She could not see her face, but she felt the dryness of a dusty schoolyard sticking to her cheeks, along with her escaped tangles.

Maybe if I sit real still, they won't see my loose braid.

Fat chance. The school board did not need a pair of field glasses to see she was a rumpled, dirty mess.

"Good afternoon, sirs." Andi stood. It was expected, come what may. "To what do we owe this pleasure?"

Pleasure, nothing! Andi knew exactly why they were here.

"We have come to assess our substitute teacher," Judge Morrison said.

Mr. Evans stepped forward and looked Andi up and down. "Just in the nick of time too, I see." He sniffed his disdain.

The board members made their way up the classroom aisle. As they neared the teacher's desk, their eyes grew wider.

Andi blushed. Just then she caught Justin's gaze. He was biting the inside of his cheek, as if trying hard not to laugh.

Not funny, big brother. Your sister has really done it this time.

"Well, Miss Carter." Mr. Evans crossed his arms over his chest. "Do you have an explanation for this . . . this complete disregard for the lack of propriety displayed here?" He waved one hand at Andi and returned to crossing his arms.

Andi ducked her head. The toe of her boot traced a pattern on the floor.

"Miss Carter?"

She looked up. "No, sir."

Justin raised a hand to his mouth and closed his eyes.

The sour-faced undertaker snorted. "I am appalled at your appearance. It no doubt reflects upon your teaching ability."

Andi winced. What a cruel, untrue shot! *That weaselly, mean-mouthed—*

She broke off her thoughts at the slight shake of Justin's head. His eyes were still closed.

Maybe he's praying for me, Andi hoped. She looked over her class. They sat mesmerized, taking it all in.

"It's a good thing we decided to stop by and check on you today," the judge added. "It's clear you have been roughhousing with your students. Much more of this nonsense, and you would quickly lose control of your classroom."

Lose control? The children were as well-behaved as if they were statues. Even Cody's creatures were silent. *Thank you, Lord!*

Andi swallowed. She'd gotten herself into this mess by giving in to the temptation to play, rather than to conduct herself as a grown-up young lady and a teacher. The seriousness of the situation suddenly overwhelmed her.

Yes, playing with the children had been the wrong choice. Mr. Evans was probably right. It might be best to confess it right away, before they accused her of something worse.

"It was just a little game of ante-over, sir. I was wrong. It won't happen again."

Mr. Bartlett, the farmer, peered closer. He whistled.

"Miss Carter, I do believe you have a rather large goose egg on your forehead."

The rest of the men stepped forward.

Justin looked concerned. "Are you all right?"

No, Andi was not all right. She would never be all right again. But she nodded. "I'm fine, Just—Mr. Carter."

Mr. Evans's face turned dark. "And how, pray tell, did you get that?" Before Andi could answer, he barked, "Romping and roughhousing in the schoolyard, I dare say."

"I'm afraid we shall have to call an emergency board meeting to discuss this issue," Judge Morrison decided.

Andi sent an appealing glance at Justin. *Help!* What would Mother say if she found out her daughter had been fired for partaking in a game of ante-over? Her cheeks flamed.

"I wouldn't call it an issue, gentleman," Justin put in. He winked at Andi. "Just a little misstep."

"A misstep?" Mr. Evans scanned Andi's loose, mussed braid, her wrinkled skirt, and her soiled shirtwaist.

"That musta been *some* misstep," Mr. Bartlett said with a chuckle.

Mr. Evans and Judge Morrison did not look amused.

"How do you intend to explain this away as a misstep, Miss Carter?"

"S'cuse me." Charley popped out of his seat. His eyes were huge. "Can I say somethin'?"

Justin smiled. "Go right ahead, young man."

"It's not An—Miss Carter's fault."

"What isn't?" Mr. Evans snapped.

"Her dirty clothes. She wasn't the least bit dirty, not the entire time. Our teacher acted like a right-proper young lady the whole noon hour."

"That's right!" Cody burst out. "She got dirty cuz—"

"Cuz she saved me!" Lillie yelled, bursting into tears.

"The ball was comin' down awful quick," Charley said. "She pushed Lillie out of the way, or she woulda been hurt real bad!"

"Is that how you got that goose egg?" Justin asked.

Andi nodded. But she was given no chance to speak.

Two more children leaped to her defense. "After Miss Carter pushed Lillie out of the way, she tried to catch the ball, but it smacked her right in the head and—"

"Down she went!" Cody finished.

"Yeah, that's right!" three others yelled.

"Thank you for speaking up," Judge Morrison said. "But that does not excuse the fact that Miss Carter was playing ante-over with you."

Silence. Lillie sniffed a few more times and grew quiet.

Mr. Wilson spoke for the first time. "What do you have to say for yourself, Miss Carter?"

Andi's cheeks flushed a deeper shade of scarlet. She clasped her hands, looked at Justin, and said, "Well, I've seen worse."

Justin laughed.

"Do you think this is a laughing matter, Mr. Carter?" Mr. Evans demanded. The four other men glared at Justin.

"No, of course not. Although there's truth in her words. We've both seen worse." His eyes twinkled. "And she did save her little pupil from severe injury."

Justin came and stood beside Andi. He whistled. "That *is* a pretty ugly bump, honey." He gave her a squeeze.

Suddenly, everything was all right. No matter what the outcome of the board's decision, Justin would back her up all the way. She smiled up at him.

"Please, sirs," Cody begged. He jumped up. "Don't dismiss Miss Carter. She's the best teacher we ever had."

All around the room, heads bobbed in agreement.

Andi's heart swelled with love and pride for her pupils. She stood straighter, strengthened by her brother's support and the cheerful looks on the children's faces.

"Let me stay, please," she said. "I promise I won't give in to the temptation to romp with my students."

Judge Morrison raised his eyebrows, but he addressed his next question to Justin. "What about it, Justin? Can you trust your sister to keep her word and not conduct herself in such a manner?"

Justin hugged Andi. "Absolutely. That goose egg will serve as an excellent reminder if such thoughts even trickle into her head. Right, honey?"

"Yes, sir!" Andi's nerves returned to normal.

Mr. Evans threw in a few more scathing remarks then turned and left. Mr. Bartlett, Mr. Wilson, and Judge Morrison hurried after him. They filed out.

Only Justin remained. The children relaxed. Andi relaxed.

Justin gave Andi one last squeeze. Then he whispered in her ear, "You've gained the loyalty of these children, Andi. That's quite an accomplishment in one week. I think you'll do." He smiled and put on his hat. "Carry on, Miss Carter," he said officially.

When Justin left, Andi dropped into her seat and buried her head in her arms. *Thank God that's over.* Then she looked up and called the children. "Let's line up for the spelling bee."

A wave of relief washed over Andi. She'd much rather be scolded for looking like an erring student than be scolded for failing to teach her pupils how to spell. Her accident had clearly distracted the school board from what was probably their original intention.

The five men had no doubt been ready to listen to the pupils recite so they could decide if the substitute teacher was doing her job.

When Lillie misspelled "Mississippi" and fell into her seat in defeat, Andi knew she'd escaped a bullet. These children simply could not spell!

***

Riley laughed his head off when Andi told him the story. "Nothing is ever dull with you around, Andi." He wiped the tears from his eyes and urged Pal home.

Luckily, Justin lived in town, so the rest of the family never heard about it.

Mother went around in a happy state the rest of the school term, knowing her youngest daughter was making a success of her short teaching career.

Andi restrained herself from any more recess romping. Instead, she turned the jump rope and cheered for the baseball games—without stepping a foot near home plate.

There were no more surprise visits from the school board, and the rest of Andi's teaching term passed uneventfully.

Virginia returned to her thirty-five pupils eight weeks later. They greeted her with joy, since Andi had warned them, "Anyone who does not welcome Miss Foster back will feel my sincere displeasure."

The following Monday, Andi donned her split skirt, plaid shirt, and practical Stetson, and saddled Shasta. Teaching school turned out to be the unforgettable experience Mother promised, all right, but Andi would never do it again.

Much too ladylike for her.

SHALL WE DANCE?

SAN JOAQUIN VALLEY, CALIFORNIA, SPRING 1886

April 10, 1885

There are only two months left to teach Riley how to dance. I mean, honestly! You'd think I was asking him to break a dozen broncs rather than learn a few simple steps for a wedding waltz.

Dancing with your brothers is fine, and Justin will certainly claim the first waltz (in Father's place), but I intend to have my new husband take me around the floor at least once!

Most importantly, I won't have him making a fool of himself . . . or of me.

A ndi Carter knew it would take some mighty fine sweet-talking, but she was bound and determined to convince Riley to learn to dance. Spring roundup was over, the calves were branded, and the bulk of the hectic spring rush had passed.

When the sun shone down bright and hot on the second Saturday in April, Andi asked Chad to give Riley the afternoon off.

For once, he agreed without asking questions. "Sure, little sister. Why not? He's worked hard for several weeks."

If Chad suspected Andi's motives, he didn't let on.

"Spend time with your fiancée," he told his wrangler.

If Riley suspected anything, he didn't let on, either. He helped tie up their picnic lunch and mounted Dakota with a spring in his step. "Where to?" he asked, smiling.

Andi wished she could ride up to her special spot. The creek now had a name, Memory Creek, and her and Riley's new house was being built plank by plank. According to the rest of the family, it was a pretty little house by a bubbling, mostly-year-round creek.

Andi wasn't allowed to see it until after she and Riley were married, but everybody assured her the house and small barn were nearly finished. *No fair!* She couldn't understand why she couldn't lend a hand.

But this was one of those times when Riley turned Chad Carter-stubborn about it. "You'll see it when we get back from our honeymoon in Yosemite," he promised whenever Andi asked for "one little peek."

Today's picnic spot was miles away from Memory Creek. It wasn't nearly as pretty as Andi's special spot, but it would have to do. By the time Andi and Riley rode (or rather, raced) to the meadow, the ground was dry enough to spread a blanket and open the wicker basket. No stream rushed by, but the grass was bright green, so bright it almost hurt her eyes.

The food softened Riley up, but he turned downright stubborn when Andi suggested that he'd better learn to waltz so he could dance at their wedding in two short months.

Riley rose to his feet. He held up both hands and backed away. "Uh-uh! I'd rather break both legs and hobble down the aisle than trip over your feet and end up looking like a fool."

"I won't dance with just my brothers, or with that rascally Johnny Wilson on my wedding day!" Andi yelled.

It was quite a stand-off. Andi jammed her hands on her hips. Riley jammed his hands on his hips, and they glared at each other.

Getting stubborn and yelling had never worked well for Andi in the past. Besides, Mitch always said you could catch more flies with honey than with vinegar.

"It's expected," she said, softening her voice. "Please? We're not getting married in a tiny church in town with a little cake and coffee afterward. It's a Circle C extravaganza."

"Whose idea was *that*?" Riley snapped.

Andi sighed. Neither Riley nor she had envisioned a fancy wedding. She would just as soon ride off to Yosemite with Riley . . . and get married along the way.

But Mother was set on sending her youngest daughter to the altar in a fine way, and the Carter brothers and sisters agreed.

Outnumbered! Andi was stuck.

So was Riley.

"You only need to learn one dance," Andi promised. "One waltz. It's easy. Take me around to the 'Blue Danube' or another piece at waltz timing, and I promise you needn't learn anything else."

She gave him a saucy look. "After that, your bride will dance with all the envious young bachelors. You can drink coffee and talk to the old ladies."

Riley looked at her darkly, but it didn't take much work for Andi to figure out he was coming around. The wheels were spinning inside his head. He clearly didn't like where those wheels might be headed—his bride dancing with all the other young men at *his* wedding.

"It's really expected?" he finally growled.

Andi nodded. Sadly, it was all too true.

Andrea Carter could not cook very well, but she knew how to dance every step ever invented: the waltz, polka, quadrille, Virginia Reel, on and on. When the Carter family went to the Governor's Ball in Sacramento every Christmas, it was expected that they knew how to dance well.

Riley scrunched up his face, clearly pondering.

Ah-ha! I have him at last, Andi thought.

That settled, he gave in.

A waltz would not take more than ten minutes to learn. Andi hummed "On the Beautiful Blue Danube" as loudly as she could and showed him the steps.

Then she showed him again. And again.

The fourth time around, Riley wrenched backward. Andi went flying. Down they went. Andi felt her face turn ten shades of red.

"What kind of step was *that*?" She staggered to her feet. *This is not going well at all.*

Riley apologized, and they started over.

Andi shook her head. How hard was a box-step waltz, for goodness' sake? "One-two-three, one-two-three. One—"

On "one," Riley stomped on top of Andi's left foot. It didn't hurt as much as the time Taffy had stepped on the same foot, but Andi yelped all the same.

It was a good thing she was wearing her working boots. Otherwise, her dear intended might have broken her toe. Or two.

"Good grief, Riley! Are you trying to cripple me?"

He started laughing. "I'm never going to figure this out."

Andi set her jaw. "Oh, yes, you are."

***

May 20, 1886

I finally agreed with Riley. He is never going to get it. He's too afraid of hurting me. He should be! My right foot has uncountable bruises. He has tripped and fallen more times than you can shake a stick at. Riley is a clever young man. He can most likely teach a colt to dance and bow and count, but he can't teach himself.

I gave up trying to teach him after two Saturdays. It was much too frustrating. Our last lesson ended in a big argument. It's not worth it, so no more dancing lessons. Thankfully, my toes have healed.

Andi's birthday dawned bright and hot. She sprang from her bed. "Eighteen years old!"

In less than a month she would become Mrs. Riley Prescott. The idea made tingles race up and down both arms. Only one thing marred her thoughts. She would not be dancing with her new husband at her wedding. *No sirree.*

Not for all the gold in California.

Andi's failure to teach Riley how to dance had hung over her all month like a dark cloud. A mixture of sorrow, anger, and frustration at his ineptitude on the dance flow threatened to ruin the joy of Andi's upcoming wedding.

No, she told herself firmly during her birthday breakfast. *I won't let that happen.* She would accept the fact that Riley Prescott was not perfect. That settled, Andi determined to enjoy her eighteenth birthday to the fullest.

Later that day, Riley grabbed Andi's hand and led her straight to the barn. "Your birthday gift is inside."

A birthday gift? From Riley?

Riley and horses went together like bread and butter, so of course the gift must be—

Andi caught her breath. A new saddle? The precious saddle she'd received years ago for her ninth birthday had burned up when Procopio and his band of cutthroats had torched the Carters' barn a little over a year ago.

Since then, Andi had contented herself with a cheap replacement. Yes, a new saddle would be most welcome!

But no. The wide, open area just inside the barn had been swept clean. Andi glanced around. No saddle anywhere. No saddle blanket. No new bridle or headstall . . . not even a hoof pick.

"Umm, where is my present?" Andi asked.

Riley chuckled. "I'm presenting you with your birthday present right now, soon-to-be-wife." He said it with a glint in his eye.

Andi was instantly on her guard. "Shall I close my eyes?"

Riley shook his head. His smile grew wider. Then, before Andi knew what was happening, he bowed and asked, "May I have this next waltz, m'lady?"

Andi bit her lip. "That's not funny." Just what she didn't need on her birthday was a bruised foot.

"I'll take that as a yes." He took Andi's hand, placed his other hand on her hip, and began to hum the "Blue Danube Waltz," swinging Andi nearly off her feet.

Andi gulped back her surprise. Every step was rhythm perfect. He led her around the inside of the small barn area, humming the entire song. He clearly knew it well by now.

When he got to the end of the song, he released her, bowed again, and straightened to his full height.

"Thank you, m'lady."

Andi couldn't breathe. "How did you learn to waltz?"

He cocked his head, and his face turned red. "When I realized how much it meant to you that we should dance a wedding waltz, well, I"—he shrugged—"I decided I'd best get myself another dancing instructor. Someone whose toes I couldn't bruise quite so easily."

Andi gaped at him. *Who could that be?*

Riley folded his arms across his chest. "Chad taught me."

Andi's jaw dropped. "Chad? And . . . and . . . *you?*"

Visions of those secret dancing lessons swirled around inside Andi's head. Oh, she would give a strongbox full of gold to have been a fly on the wall during those sessions.

A gush of laughter escaped her throat. She couldn't hold it back. "You and Chad . . . *waltzing.* That is the most—"

Riley clapped a hand over Andi's mouth. He leaned close to her ear and whispered, "If you *ever* let on to a single soul, especially to Chad, I'll . . . I'll—"

Andi tore his hand away and burst into another round of laughter. She shook her head. "I won't. I promise. Because not only *you* would come after me, but Chad would too. It will be our secret."

Andi, Riley, and Chad kept their secret for the rest of their lives. And Riley danced divinely at his wedding.

Thanks to Chad.

Part 2: Marriage 1886+

YOSEMITE NIGHTMARE

CIRCLE C RANCH, CALIFORNIA, JUNE 12, 1886
Note: This story opens the day *Courageous Love* ends.

More than anything, I wish all the party and celebration would end soon. What bride should go around in a snow-white wedding gown at a barbeque, for goodness sake?

Chapter 1

Andrea Carter's wedding day had turned blistering hot. It was too hot to wear stays, long sleeves, and a dress with a train that probably weighed five pounds. She'd hiked it up earlier, but it looked silly slung over her arm.

Yet, when Mother glanced her way and smiled, Andi made sure she returned the smile. *I want out of these hot, sticky clothes and into something practical—like a split skirt and a light-weight blouse. And a hat.*

Most definitely a hat, instead of the flimsy veil that kept blowing in her eyes.

"You look beautiful today, Mrs. Prescott." Riley slid onto the bench beside her and squeezed her hand. "I'm happy just to sit here and look at you."

Heat jumped into Andi's cheeks before she could order her emotions back into a corner. *Mrs. Prescott?* That sounded like an old lady, not an eighteen-year-old girl.

But Riley sure seemed to get a kick out of saying it. He'd called her *Mrs. Prescott* about a dozen times, ever since the ceremony ended two hours ago.

A stray thought tickled Andi's mind before she could order it away. *What have I gotten myself into?*

Yesterday she'd been a free and laughing young girl. Andi and Shasta had ridden all over the ranch from dawn to dusk. Her only worry was wondering if her big brother Chad would find something to boss her about.

Andi smiled. At least that part of her life was over. No more big-brother bossing!

Riley chuckled. "What are you smiling about?"

"Chad can't ever boss me again."

His eyebrows shot up. "*That's* what you're thinking about on your wedding day?" He burst out laughing.

Andi felt the heat in her cheeks spread over her entire face and down her neck. Good thing the sun was hot and bright. It would look like a sunburn.

She ducked her head.

Riley put his arm around her and squeezed. "Sorry, darling. I couldn't help it. You always make me laugh. Don't ever change, Andi. I want you to make me laugh every day."

That shouldn't be too hard, Andi thought. It didn't take much to make life-loving Riley Prescott break into a smile.

"All right," she promised. "Just so long as you promise never to boss me. I've had that for eighteen years, and I'm done with it."

"Cross my heart," Riley said solemnly. "I love you too much to boss you."

"I love you too," Andi whispered.

She peeked around her new husband and studied the crowd. They were laughing and eating and dancing. And such dancing! The Mexican music had reached a fever pitch. Old Diego strummed his guitar like he was young again.

It was all very nice, but . . . "When can we leave?"

Riley shook his head. "I dunno. Nobody told me the rules for how long the bride and groom have to stick around." He let out a breath. "I've met every friend and relative you have."

"I've met all of *your* relatives too," Andi said. "Half the soldiers from all those Army forts you lived at showed up for the party. In uniform." She giggled. "I was sure there must be an Indian uprising somewhere."

Although Andi and Riley's wedding ceremony had been a quiet affair for family and close friends only, the barbeque afterward had been opened to a huge crowd of well-wishers. She suspected most of the guests had shown up for the food, the music, and the dancing rather than to congratulate the bride and groom on their new life together.

She shook her head to chase away that thought.

The good news was they all brought wedding gifts. That would really help when Andi set up housekeeping a couple of weeks from now. She couldn't wait to see the house Riley and a dozen others had been working on since spring.

No peeking, everybody said. She'd obeyed. Soon she'd see it at last! But first . . . *Yosemite, here we come.*

Andi had never been to Yosemite. Ranch life was too busy. She would rather explore the ranch than visit what would soon become—if the government in Washington had its way—a National Park.

Whatever *that* was. Hopefully it meant people would take better care of the place.

As far as a honeymoon was concerned, if she had to choose between Yosemite and San Francisco, the mountains would win any day over the city. Melinda had sung the praises of her honeymoon week in San Francisco. The opera! The Palace Hotel! The restaurants—

Andi shook her head. Not San Francisco!

The city by the Bay held no good memories for the youngest Carter. It would be the last place Andi would choose for a wedding trip destination.

She squinted up at the afternoon sun. A few more hours and she and Riley could get out of here and be on their way.

Chad strolled up just then. Grinning, he ripped her away from her spot on the bench. "I haven't had a spare moment to wish you congratulations, little sister."

He held her out at arm's length. "You know, of course, that Justin and I had to arm wrestle to see who won the privilege of walking you down the aisle in Father's place."

Andi smirked. It had never been a contest. Justin would do it. He'd been playing Father for over ten years.

Chad pulled her into a hug. "I'm going to miss you."

"I'm not moving back east," Andi huffed. "Only less than an hour's ride on a fast—or even slow—horse."

"Ah, but you are so much easier to tease when we're living under the same roof."

No doubt.

The music started up again, and Chad swung Andi into the dance circle. "One more dance," he said, kissing the top of her head. "For luck."

***

Finally! Out of these hot, heavy silks. Andi let out a long, relieved sigh. It felt lovely to be back in her familiar split skirt and blouse. They were excellent traveling clothes.

Good-bye to the bothersome veil. Good riddance to the stiff, hot bun that had rested on the top of her head. She plaited her mass of nearly black waves into one long braid.

"There," she declared to the floor-length mirror. "Back to the Andi that Riley knows and loves."

Before she could look away, she spied the reflection of a gold ring encircling her finger. A deep-blue sapphire with diamond chips on either side sparkled.

How funny it feels. A shiver passed through her. *This is scary. Was it only this morning when I was young, headstrong Andi Carter? Now I'm . . .* She gulped. *Mrs. Andrea Carter Prescott.*

Andi sucked in a deep breath. *I can hardly believe this. I was so impatient for the year to go by. So anxious for this day. And now I'm a married woman.*

Speaking of which, wasn't this bride's groom waiting for her downstairs?

Andi looked around one last time. This morning she'd done the same thing, until Kate came looking for her. Andi thought this morning would be the last time she lingered in her childhood room. But no. She'd forgotten she had to change, so here she was. One last time.

This was the Circle C ranch. Her home. Even if she returned to visit, this would no longer be her room.

"Don't be silly," she scolded herself. "Riley and I have a house of our own. That will be my home."

But Andi couldn't stop shaking. She had just taken a major step in her life. What was it she'd written in her journal just this morning?

I will always remember June 12, 1886, as my most memorable milestone.

She took another deep breath. *I didn't trip on the stairs. The wedding ceremony went well. I felt fine. The reception was wonderful. So, why am I having such a wave of anxiety?*

No time for further musing. Her guests were waiting downstairs. She and Riley must say their good-byes. She squared her shoulders and left the room.

***

"Good-bye, Mother." Andi hugged her tight. "See you in two weeks."

"Yes, sweetheart. Have fun." Mother swiped at her eyes and returned the embrace. "Riley," she addressed the smiling young man, "take care of my daughter now, do you hear?"

Riley nodded. "Yes, ma'am. With pleasure."

Chad laughed and slapped Riley on the back. "You have quite a task, brother-in-law. You sure you're up to it?"

"Oh, yes." Riley's eyes twinkled. "Most definitely."

When Mother finally released her daughter, Chad gave Andi a hug. "Be good for your husband, baby sister," he said softly, ruffling her hair.

Andi wriggled away. "One more order for the road, huh, Chad? If you recall, you're not my boss any longer."

Chad chuckled. "Nope, but Riley might need to call on my assistance sometime soon. You might be too much for him to handle alone."

"Don't count on it."

After finishing dozens of good-byes, Andi followed Riley outside. A ranch hand had hitched up the buggy. Riley helped Andi climb in then swung up beside her.

"I'll leave the buggy at the livery," he told Chad.

"Get going, you two!" Chad waved them away. "You don't want to miss the train."

Chapter 2

MADERA, CALIFORNIA, JUNE 13, 1886

Today is my first full day of being Mrs. Andrea Prescott. It's starting off as a marvelous adventure, if only I wasn't so tired.

"Wake up, Andi."

A gentle shake made Andi snuggle down deeper under the quilt. "Go away."

Andi knew what would happen next. One of her brothers would throw a glass of water on her head. She didn't care. She was so tired she kept her eyes tightly closed.

When no water splashed her face, she opened one eye—and gasped.

Riley sat on the bed next to her. "We're not going to catch that stagecoach to Yosemite if you don't get a move-on."

Andi blinked. Visions of being rousted from bed for school flew from her head.

She hadn't been in school for over a year. Well, if she didn't count her short term as a substitute teacher last winter.

Her mind cleared. No more school! Not ever. No more mean brothers trying to pull her out of bed on school days. No more icy water in her face.

Hurrah!

She was so happy she sat up and flung her arms around Riley's neck. "What time is it?"

"Five-fifteen." He untangled Andi's arms and stood up. A few strides took him to the window, where he flung the curtains aside.

"The sun's been up half an hour already," he announced.

"Stage leaves at six-thirty."

Andi's exhaustion from the day before overwhelmed her just then. She fell back against the soft pillows. She barely remembered the rest of party, or even the train trip. Andi had gone around in a fog, doing whatever anyone had told her.

Even the half-hour train ride from Fresno to Madera last night was a mist.

"We don't have to go if you're all tuckered out," Riley said. "We can hang around in Madera." He pressed his nose against the window. "Though, I'm not thinking there's much to do or see here."

"No, I'm fine." She threw off the bedcovers and hurried to the washroom to splash water on her face and get ready.

This really was a fancy hotel. A private washroom instead of a washroom down the hall that all the guests shared?

Heavens! It must have cost a fortune, Andi mused. *Reckon that's why they call it the bridal suite?*

Whatever the reason, Andi was glad she didn't have to tromp down the hotel hallway in her dressing gown.

Yes sirree! This was much better.

Andi didn't know how long it took other young ladies to wash, dress, and do up their hair, but she managed it in fifteen minutes.

She even let her thick, dark braid hang down her back. All too soon some stuffy old matron would tell her to put it up, now that she was a married woman, but until then she could avoid a headache.

Besides, Riley liked Andi's hair down. "What's the point of putting all that lovely hair up where nobody can see it?" he'd complained more than once after a Sunday service.

Very forward thinking, that man.

Riley had clearly been up for at least an hour.

He was shaved and dressed in his familiar duds—long-sleeved shirt, dungarees, high-topped (what some citified people called "cowboy") boots, and a vest to hold odds and ends. His waist sported a shiny silver buckle and new leather belt, Andi's wedding gift to him. His jacket lay slung over a chair.

The newlyweds breakfasted in the hotel dining room, along with eight or nine other people who were obviously headed up into the mountains. An older gentleman and his wife, both white-haired and jolly-looking, chatted at the table next to Andi and Riley.

Across the room, two other couples ate heartily. It wasn't hard to overhear their conversation.

"Oh, do you think we'll be robbed on this trip?" a woman with tightly pulled-back hair and a pouting lower lip asked the waiter as he served them.

"Oh, no, madam. There is no danger at all."

The woman's mouth showed even more of a pout. "Oh, I do wish we would."

Andi rolled her eyes at the silly comment. Who would wish to be robbed? She caught Riley's amused grin.

Greenhorns, he mouthed.

Just like everyone else for miles around, Andi knew the stories. The Yosemite stage had its share of mishaps. Road agents hid and waited, usually where the coach had to slow down at the mountain curves.

Then they popped out and demanded the strongbox. They also took watches, rings, money, and even buttons.

But that was all the highwaymen ever did.

One would think that the reports that showed up weekly in the *Expositor* during the tourist season would scare visitors away. Instead, the incidents were looked on as romantic.

Adventure for the city folks, Andi thought with a giggle.

The idea of a romantic encounter with a real, live robber in the dark forests surrounding a mountain road clearly added excitement to the women's otherwise dreary lives.

"Be assured, Miss Amber," the woman's tall, blond, male companion was saying. "I and the other gentlemen aboard the stage will certainly be on the alert, prepared for any kind of terrible confrontation."

Riley stifled a snort.

Andi nearly choked on her orange juice. "Time to go," she whispered, "before I back out."

Riley frowned, puzzled. "You scared of getting held up?"

"Not at all. I just might not want to spend six long hours stuffed in a stagecoach with this present company."

Riley rose and helped Andi with her chair.

"You'll be one of those gallant young show-offs to come to our rescue, won't you, Sir Galahad?" Andi quipped.

"Indeed I will, my princess."

Chuckling, Riley and Andi left the dining room. They were first in line on the porch when the Yosemite Stage and Turnpike coach rolled to a stop in front of the hotel.

The coach was spanking clean and looked brand-new, with bright-red paint and large, red-and-yellow spoked wheels. However, it wasn't quite like the other stagecoaches Andi had seen and ridden in during her life.

There were no doors. Instead, the sides lay wide open to the air . . . *and the dust and dirt*, Andi thought.

"Step right up, folks," the driver called from the wide seat high above the passengers.

Andi stepped into the coach. Three rows faced forward. Each bench seat looked like it could hold four passengers, or five in a pinch.

Another man stashed everyone's luggage in a boot at the back of the coach, for this was not a day trip. By the time the stage pulled into the Mariposa Grove six hours later, the passengers would be too tired from rattling and bumping around to *ooh* and *ahh* at the giant sequoias.

One needed a good night's sleep to appreciate Yosemite.

Riley found seats for himself and Andi in the first row, just behind the driver. "Less jarring," he whispered in her ear.

Andi nodded and looked out. She had a sudden urge to ask Riley to trade places with her. There was no door, and no sturdy sides. If the horses raced around a curve, she might be tossed out like the end boy in a game of crack-the-whip.

A man with a moustache and hair that curled around his ears settled himself next to Riley. "Howdy."

"Howdy yourself," Riley answered.

The man leaned back. "First time up to the Valley?"

Riley nodded. "But we've heard lots about it. You been there before?"

"I live there," he replied. "Just came down to Madera on business and now I'm headed back. Hope I don't have to come down here again. I prefer my job as caretaker of the hotel up there."

"Hey, Sam!" The driver poked his head through the opening. "Mind riding up top with me? Got extra passengers this trip."

The man sighed. "Reckon so, Tad." He tipped his hat to Andi. "Have a good trip, ma'am, sir."

Chapter 3

THE YOSEMITE STAGE, CALIFORNIA, JUNE 13, 1886

It took me less than ten minutes to remember how awful it is to ride in a stagecoach. What was I thinking when I begged to go to Yosemite for our honeymoon?

I forgot how rough a ride these stagecoaches give a person." Andi shifted for the dozenth time in her uncomfortable seat. "I can't believe we paid forty-five dollars each for the privilege of being churned like butter."

"What a crazy way to spend a honeymoon!"

Melinda's laughing voice echoed in Andi's head. For once, Andi was beginning to agree. A horseback trek to the Yosemite Valley would be much more to her liking than this rattling sardine can.

A vision of a flat can of sardines made her giggle. Every spot on the coach was filled. Two male passengers sat up top, squeezed in next to the driver. Inside, the rest were all laid out like sardines, with not a speck of free space to stretch out.

Two young men sat next to Andi and Riley on their front-row seat. The man closest to the far edge of the coach had rusty-red hair, a shaven face, and a quick smile. He pulled out his harmonica and played a jaunty tune to pass the time.

Just behind them on the second row, the two couples from breakfast laughed and joked. "We sure don't have holidays like this in Chicago," one gentleman quipped.

"It is quite exciting," the young lady named Amber agreed.

The back seat held the older couple. They hadn't said a word the entire trip, at least as far as Andi could tell. They were hemmed in on either side by two older, business-type men.

One was a portly fellow, carrying a flat case. He held it tightly on his lap.

That was the only glimpse Andi had of the crowded coach. It was hard to catch conversation over the rattling and banging. *Someday, they really ought to run a railroad track up here.*

Four long, bumpy hours later, Riley's hand encircled Andi's waist. "Hold on. We're coming to another curve." He peered past the two young men sitting near the opposite side and whistled. "Looks like a hairpin turn too."

Great. Andi shifted her weight away from the open doorway, planted her feet, and leaned against Riley. The horses slowed down. Not only was it a hairpin turn, but it was also uphill.

The worse turn so far.

"This steep road shows we are almost to Yosemite," Riley explained cheerfully.

The coach's front wheel hit a rock in the road, jarring the coach and jolting the passengers. They yelped and shifted.

"Sorry about that, folks," the driver called from above. "We'll be there in an hour or so. The Valley is worth the ride. Hang on."

Andi grasped the supporting pole next to her seat. *If we live to see it*, she thought with a groan.

Another tune poured out from the harmonica-playing young man. The tune made Andi smile. She'd heard the song many times before.

Creeping through the valley, crawling o'er the hill,
Splashing through the branches, rumbling o'er the mill;
Putting nervous gentlemen in a towering rage.
What is so provoking as riding in a stage?

Andi hummed along through the rest of the song. Some fellow had taken the verses of an old Southern tune "Goober Peas" and composed an accurate description of stagecoach travel.

"Isn't it delightful, riding in a stage?"

Andi winced as a wheel banged over a rock.

It was definitely *not* delightful!

The stage successfully rounded the curve, but no one was given time to breathe sighs of relief.

"Whoa!" the driver shouted.

Andi and Riley looked at each other as the stage came to a skidding, dusty, clattering standstill.

"Landslide?" one of the passengers wondered aloud.

It was a reasonable cause for delay. The steep mountain slopes were always giving way to boulders large and small. They tumbled down the mountainside and landed in the road.

Andi slumped in her seat. "Are we never going to get there?"

"Patience, sweetheart," Riley whispered in her ear. "This is part of the adventure."

"I reckon." But Andi was ready for supper and rest.

The noon dinner stop in Fresno Flats was now only a dim memory. Andi leaned out her side of the coach. "I wonder how much of a pile—"

She caught her breath. Her stomach turned over. It wasn't a landslide. It wasn't a downed tree across the road.

It was two masked men.

Chapter 4

SIERRA WILDERNESS, CALIFORNIA, JUNE 13, 1886

Unbelievable! Amber's silly wish has come true. Our stagecoach is being held up.

Andi's throat felt dryer than the dust swirling around the carriage. Two masked men stood in the middle of the roadway, only yards away from the stomping, snorting horses. Both men were dressed in black and wore their clothes wrong side out.

The smaller man was armed with a shotgun, but it was the tall man who grabbed Andi's attention. He held a .44 Colt pistol, and it looked like he knew how to use it.

This fellow meant business.

Andi swallowed and tried to make herself small. "The stage is being held up," she whispered to Riley.

His eyes widened. His fingers found hers, and he squeezed. "Stay calm. If we do what they say, they'll let us go on our way." He smiled, but his hazel eyes were dark with concern.

When the horses had settled down, the taller of the two men hollered, "All right, everybody out!"

From the seat behind Andi, Amber gushed, "A robbery. A real-live robbery. How romantic!" She tittered and pretended to swoon.

Andi rolled her eyes and sighed. Foolish young woman. There was nothing romantic about being robbed at gunpoint in the middle of nowhere.

The tall highwayman stomped to the coach's open side. "I said"—he yanked Andi's arm—"out!"

Andi flew from the stage.

She caught her balance just in time, pushed herself away from the man, and scowled. "Leave me alone."

He backed away and raised his pistol. "Shut up, miss, and you won't get hurt."

Andi shut up. But she couldn't help staring. There was something familiar about this road agent's voice.

Now, where have I heard it before? She peered up at him.

To her surprise, the highwayman's brown eyes behind his mask opened wide. "*Get moving,*" he barked, motioning Andi to stand clear of the carriage.

Riley sprang from the stage and put his arm around Andi's waist. "We'll do whatever you say. Rob us and be on your way."

The highwayman jabbed his pistol into Riley's chest. "*I'm* giving the orders here, mister."

Andi bit her lip. *I should know him.* Her thoughts whirled.

The robber poked his head inside the coach and waved his pistol around. "Everybody. Out. Now."

The short man with the shotgun motioned the driver and the other two men down from up top. "Throw down the box," he demanded.

Thunk!

The heavy Wells Fargo strong box landed in the road. It no doubt held the payroll for any loggers or other businesses up near Yosemite.

The tall road agent lined the fourteen passengers and the driver up against the stagecoach. "Empty your pockets." He removed his wide Stetson and tossed it on the ground. "Toss the money into the hat . . . and be quick about it."

With frantic jingling, the hat began to fill up.

"You ladies," the man said. "Take off your charms, your bracelets and brooches, rings, and other jewelry and put them in the hat with the cash."

Amber yanked the earrings from her lobes.

"That's right," the man said. "Keep 'em comin'."

Amber dropped her earrings into the hat. When she passed the road agent, she batted her eyelashes at him. "I do hope you won't hurt us," she murmured.

"Shut up." He reached out and yanked a diamond-studded brooch from the lace at Amber's throat. "Don't forget this, ma'am." He chuckled and tossed it in the hat.

Amber pressed her lips together and returned to the arm of her companion.

The hat filled up. Male passengers added their wallets and watches and cuff links. When the road agent waved his gun in front of Riley's belt, he sighed and began to remove the silver buckle.

Andi choked back a shout. Not Riley's brand-new silver belt buckle! He'd worn her wedding gift to him for only one day. She opened her mouth to protest, but Riley shook his head.

He looped the belt and lowered it into the hat.

Shorty dropped his Stetson on the ground. "Quite a haul today, eh, Big T? Gonna need another hat, ain't we?"

The tall one, Big T, grunted. "Please, your buttons too."

Gasps came from the passengers.

He laughed. "Not from the ladies' frocks, but the sleeve buttons of you gents. I see some of them are pearls." He singled out the older couple. "Hurry up."

The older gentleman was clearly a rich man. He popped his shirt and sleeve buttons off and dropped them into the hat. His wife sobbed quietly. She looked ready to keel over.

Andi's blood boiled. How dare they terrorize an old man and an old woman! She clenched her fists.

"You there," Shorty demanded.

Andi whirled.

"Yes, *you*." He nodded at her hands, which were clasped in front of her split skirt. "Hold out your hands."

Andi's stomach turned over, but she did what she was told. Sparkling in the sunlight, her brand-new wedding band—the one with the pretty blue sapphire and tiny diamonds—came into full view.

Big T whistled. "Now, that's what I call a prize."

"Hand it over," Shorty growled.

Andi thrust her hands behind her back. *No!* she screamed silently. *Never!*

She'd had this ring on her finger for little over one day. She'd told herself she would never take it off.

"Andi," Riley said firmly. "Give the man your ring." He lowered his voice. "Now."

The tall road agent jerked his head around at her name. His eyes narrowed through the mask's holes, as if something he'd guessed had been right.

He turned to Shorty. "We've got enough treasure. I don't need the ring." He chuckled. "I wouldn't want to cut off her finger to get it."

Not funny, Andi thought.

He motioned toward their horses. "Let's—"

Bang! A gun went off.

The ladies screamed. Andi and Riley dove for cover.

Andi raised her head in time to see the portly gentleman who'd carried his flat case on his lap dig into his valise and yank out another small derringer.

The shotgun went off, and the man dropped to the ground.

Andi squeezed her eyes shut. *He's dead!*

"Fool," the short highwayman muttered. He walked over and grabbed the valise. "These are right-nice derringers."

The road agent should not have turned his back.

"Let's overpower them, men!" the driver shouted. "It's fifteen to two."

Leaping forward, the stage driver and two of the passengers went for the highwaymen. The driver snaked an arm around Shorty and began to wrestle him for the shotgun.

Big T moved like lightning. Before either Andi or Riley had a chance to react, Big T reached down and grabbed Andi by the arm. Pulling her to her feet, he jammed his pistol against her temple.

She winced.

"That's enough," Big T barked. "Let my partner go."

Chapter 5

Andi's heart thudded. Anger, despair, and a sick feeling in her stomach all swirled together. A hot flush worked its way up her neck.

How dare he! Without thinking about the consequences, she doubled over and shrieked in false pain.

The man pulled away the pistol, but he didn't let go of her arm. "What in tarnation's wrong with you?"

By now, Shorty had been released. He smacked the man who'd tackled him and hurried over to the tall road agent's side. "These folks are crazy, all of them."

Andi didn't respond to either of the men's words. At least not vocally. Mustering all her strength and courage, Andi elbowed the tall one in the stomach. When he released her to clutch his belly, Andi reached up. She grabbed his mask and ripped it away.

The face beneath the disguise made her gasp. "Troy!"

It couldn't be, but it was.

Her sister's outlaw husband was at it again. How long had it been? Six years? Hadn't the man learned anything?

Troy swore and reached for his mask.

"Too late for that now, Big T," Shorty muttered.

Breathing hard, Andi backstepped until she fell into Riley.

He closed her in a tight embrace. "Of all the ridiculous stunts," he whispered. "You could have been killed."

Troy stood frozen. He seemed to have forgotten about his robbery. His brow was furrowed, his gun clasped tightly in one hand. But it was pointed at the ground.

"Yeah, Andi," he admitted. "It's me."

"How *could* you?" Andi burst out. "When you rode off that day at the creek, you had the perfect chance to turn your life around. You could have gone back to Kate and the kids. I know they miss you. Why did you—"

"Shut up!"

Andi's mouth snapped shut.

"No more surprises." Troy waved the gun around. "I've had a bellyful of unwanted shocks. First, the gunshot. Now this." He looked disgusted.

A moan came from the portly man on the ground.

Andi's heart leaped. The man was alive. But probably not for long, not here in the middle of nowhere.

"Look what you did, Troy! I never took you for a killer. A swindler and an outlaw, yes. But not"—Andi waved her hand toward the man—"this."

"Yelling at him won't get us out of this fix," Riley said.

"Have you any idea who this road agent is?" Andi snapped.

Riley shook his head.

"Troy Swanson."

Riley's mouth fell open. "Your brother-in-law?"

"*Former* brother-in-law," Andi said. "We disowned him six years ago. I haven't seen him since."

Troy glowered at her. "If it were up to me, you wouldn't be seeing me now, either."

"Does any of this matter?" The older gentleman stepped up. "Mr. Henry is in great agony. He needs attention before he bleeds to death. He needs a doctor."

The gentleman's wife lowered herself next to Mr. Henry. Her face was pale, but she hadn't swooned. She examined him briefly then faced Troy. "Please, sir. I was a nurse during the War. Let me help him."

Troy and Shorty exchanged glances. Shorty shrugged.

"We're about an hour's ride from our destination. They have a doctor there," the driver put in.

Troy chewed on his lower lip before speaking. "Here's what you're going to do," he finally said. "Some of you load Mr. Henry onto the stage. Then all of you men will accompany him to Wawona. I don't want to be hounded by the law for murder." He looked pale and uncertain.

Andi relaxed. "Thank you, Troy," she said softly.

"Don't thank me yet." He pointed his pistol at Amber, the other young lady, and Andi. "The nurse can go along to tend Mr. Henry. You three ladies will stay with Shorty and me. By the time the men return, we'll be gone. We'll leave the ladies behind. They'll be tired and cold, but still here."

"Over my dead body," yelled the young dandy.

Troy stepped up and slammed the man's face with the butt of his pistol. He dropped like a stone and was silent.

Andi looked at Riley. He was simmering in rage and fear. Fear for Andi's safety.

"We'll be all right," she told him. "I know Troy. He won't hurt us." *I hope.*

When Riley didn't answer, Andi urged him, "Hurry, before Mr. Henry dies. Troy will have no reason to keep us alive if the man dies and he's marked as a killer."

Troy smirked at Riley. "Who is that fellow, anyway? You know him?"

Andi gave Troy a stiff nod. "A friend."

She didn't elaborate. It was none of his business.

Silence fell.

"Get going!" Troy burst out. "It's getting late."

Three men carried the limp and bleeding Mr. Henry into the coach and laid him on the front bench. The older woman climbed up beside him. She held a cloth against the chest wound. Her lips moved in silent prayer.

The rest of the men reluctantly joined her. The driver climbed up into his seat. "Giddup." The horses took off.

The last look Andi had of her new husband was his worried face peering out of the carriage. He waved. *I love you,* he mouthed. *Stay safe.*

Andi heart turned over. *Will I ever see Riley again?*

Chapter 6

The coach disappeared around a curve in a cloud of dust. Amber burst into tears. "Oh, Martha, what is going to become of us?"

Not so romantic now, is it? Andi didn't voice her thoughts. That would be unkind. She felt sorry for the two citified women. She felt sorry for herself. *How will we get out of this fix?*

She turned to Troy. "Were you telling the truth when you said you'll leave us here and go on your way?"

Shorty snorted. "No—"

"Yes," Troy cut Shorty off. "I don't want three weeping—I mean *two* weeping—women around our necks. They'll just slow us down." He gave Amber and Martha a disgusted look. "Stop blubbering."

The women threw their arms around each other and collapsed to the ground. Their cries turned to muffled gasps.

Shorty squatted next to the hats and started transferring the loot into a rough burlap sack. "You're gettin' soft, Big T," he muttered. He shook his head and kept scooping.

Troy ignored him. He took Andi's arm and led her a little distance from his grouchy partner and the weeping women. "Sit down."

Andi sat.

To her surprise, Troy joined her on the ground. "Really, Andi, we're only keeping you here until we know the stage has gone on to Wawona. I don't want any sneaky passengers jumping off the coach and coming back to capture us . . . or any other fool heroics. Shorty and I will be on our way as soon as it's full dark."

Andi grunted. She wasn't sure she believed him.

Troy sighed. "I reckon you're wondering why I'm here."

To rob stagecoaches, Andi was tempted to shout. She took a deep breath. *Please, God, guard my tongue.* "Yes, the thought did cross my mind."

He looked at the ground. "After I left you and the kids under that tree all those years ago, I debated turning myself in. I thought that a short prison term—or even a long one—would be worth returning to a better life. When I got out, I could settle down with my wife and kids in San Francisco and find another way to make a living."

"Why didn't you?" Andi's heart turned over.

Troy shrugged. "I couldn't."

Andi waited. Stinging, accusing words rose to her lips, but she swallowed them. A quiet voice warned her to be silent.

A few minutes later, Troy went on. "I made it out of the hills and to Madera. I figured the law was after me, so I made myself scarce." He shrugged. "I panicked. I didn't want to pay the price of turning myself in."

He shook his head. "I couldn't see myself behind bars."

Andi sighed inwardly. If Troy had turned himself in back then, he would probably have been released by now. Robbery didn't carry as stiff a penalty as murder or kidnapping.

She looked into his eyes. She didn't need to tell him what he clearly knew already.

"In the end, my current life seemed best. Robbing stages is easy pickings. Especially up here." Troy nodded toward the forested slopes that rose on either side. "Lonely place, this Yosemite road." He chuckled. "And we've got the reputation of never hurting anyone."

"Until now," Andi reminded him.

He nodded. "Fool. If he'd kept the derringers in his case, we'd be gone. You would all be nearly to Wawona by now and enjoying your camping trip in the Valley."

A strange expression covered his face. He wrinkled his forehead. "Hold on a minute. I saw only you on that stage. No brothers. No escort. Just that young fella."

He narrowed his eyes. "Isn't that a rather improper thing for Andrea Carter to do? To go traipsing off to the wilderness without a family companion, and in the company of a young man?"

He grinned. "I'm surprised at you."

Andi ducked her head and clasped her hands around her knees. She didn't say a word.

Troy's eyebrows rose. "Wait a minute." His smile grew wider. He grabbed her hand. "Is this what I think it is?"

Andi jerked her hand away. Troy had let her keep her ring, but he'd apparently only made the connection this minute.

He whistled. "The dark-haired fellow who donated his silver belt buckle?"

Andi nodded but kept her head bowed. Heat was creeping into her cheeks, and she couldn't stop it. Why was Troy teasing her about being married?

"What's his name?" he asked.

None of your business, Andi snapped silently. "Riley Prescott," she murmured.

"Huh." Troy grunted. "He looks mighty young. I can't believe those brothers of yours let you marry him. Nobody's good enough for a Carter girl." He sounded bitter.

Andi looked up. "Riley's been Chad's top wrangler for two years. Now, we have our own place." Her voice dropped. "We were married yesterday."

"Is that a fact!" He chuckled.

Andi's blood boiled at his lightheartedness at her expense. "Yes. We were on our way to the Valley for our honeymoon when you showed up."

"What did you intend to do there?"

"Rent some horses and go camping in the Valley." Andi felt her eyes light up. Then she drooped. "I reckon the whole trip is ruined now."

Troy scratched at his stubble. "How was I supposed to know you were on that stage?"

Andi shrugged and said nothing.

Troy sighed. "How are Kate and the kids?"

"Fine. Levi is as tall as Mitch now and has really filled out. He comes out to the ranch every summer to help Chad."

She smiled. "He's a handsome boy, Troy."

"You don't say!" He grinned.

"He looks just like you. Brown eyes, brown hair. The girls have turned into young ladies. Betsy is nearly thirteen and Hannah is ten."

Troy's his face showed his longing.

"I think they miss having a father around." Andi took a big breath. "Why don't you go to the city and see them?"

Troy shook his head. "Nah. By now, Katie's probably found some other fellow—an honest, upstanding one."

"No, she hasn't," Andi told him. "She's staying faithful to her marriage vows. She won't ever marry. She's focusing on raising the children. They're going to turn out well."

"Good to hear." Troy picked up a stick and tossed it into the forest.

"She loves you Troy," Andi said. "I can't imagine why, but she does."

Troy grew silent.

"I thought—I *hoped*—you'd think about life and turning to God. Maybe even owning up to the crimes you've committed." Andi took a deep breath. "You still could, you know. When I go home, I'm going to tell Kate I saw you. That I talked to you. What shall I tell her?"

Troy's eyes flashed. He stood up suddenly and marched over to the loot. With a sweep of his hand, he yanked the silver buckle and belt from the burlap sack.

"What the—"

"Shut up, Shorty," Troy told his companion.

Shorty shut up. There was no doubt about who was boss.

Troy walked over to Andi and dropped the belt and buckle in her lap. "Congratulations on gettin' hitched," he said. "Consider this a wedding gift."

Andi clutched the belt and did not say thank you.

Troy squatted down beside her. "Listen, Andi. If that fellow we shot lives, I'll turn myself in. If he doesn't live, I can never give myself up. You understand, don't you?"

Andi said nothing, but she was silently praying, *Lord, keep the derringer salesman alive!*

Troy's voice dropped to a whisper. "Tell Kate I love her. I didn't know how much until I lost her. I reckon it's all my fault, and I see that now." He drew a deep breath. "Tell the kids I-I . . . well, tell them I'm sorry. I'll come back when I straighten all this out."

"Will I be telling them the truth?" Andi held Troy's dark-brown gaze.

He nodded and rose. "Shorty," he called. "Let's get outta here."

Chapter 7

Shorty slung the burlap sack over his shoulder and started for his horse. Troy followed. There was a lot of yelling and arguing, but when the two men rode off, the burlap sack remained on the ground.

Andi, Martha, and Amber ran to it. Darkness had fallen, but there was enough light from a rising moon to see that the road agents had left the loot behind.

Amber gasped her surprise and fished out her brooch. "My stars! Why ever would those two villains do such a thing? They robbed us, and then they gave it back?"

Martha's eyes were huge. "I don't understand."

Andi did. She smiled in the growing darkness. It was the first step toward Troy's redemption.

"It's way past nightfall," she told the women. "We're free from the robbers, but we'd better find shelter." Highwaymen weren't the only dangers on this wilderness road.

Amber's jaw dropped. "W-we're alone?" Her voice shook. "In the middle of—"

"I'm sure the men will be back for us as soon as they can," Andi assured the shaking young woman. She pointed to a grassy area under a large pine tree. "There."

Grasping hands, Amber and Martha followed Andi off the road. "What about wild beasts?" Martha asked.

Andi shrugged. "What about them?" Her insides quaked, but she didn't want frightened, shrieking women to call the hungry predators to their front door.

"What will we do?" Amber whispered.

"I'll light a fire," Andi told her. "Just a small one, but it will be enough to keep coyotes and other creatures away. None of them care for a blaze."

"You can do that?" Martha gaped at her.

Andi reached into her split skirt's wide pocket and drew out two items. "I never go anywhere in the backcountry without a tin of matches and a pocketknife."

Amber's giggle sounded high-pitched and nervous. "You carry around a *knife?*"

"Oh, yes. My brother Mitch gave it to me for my twelfth birthday. It's often come in handy."

A long-ago memory tickled Andi's mind. Mitch shot, helpless. Her knife cutting away his blood-soaked trousers. She shivered.

The women didn't reply.

Andi sent them for pine needles and dry lichen, as well as small, dead branches. In no time, she had kindled a small, hot fire. "Now we wait."

"For how long?" Amber inquired.

Andi shrugged. "Until somebody comes for us, or until daylight. Then we walk."

To fill the lonely hours, Andi asked Amber and Martha to share stories about their lives. It was a kind act, one Andi wished she hadn't undertaken. She was stuck listening to the girls' accounts of balls, the opera, and their travels to Europe.

But it worked in calming the women down. When they asked Andi what her plans were, she grinned. "Riley and I are on our honeymoon. We're going camping in the Valley."

She chuckled at their open-mouthed astonishment. "So you see, this campfire was just the beginning."

Much later, when a bright half-moon stood high overhead and cast its silver light on the road, Andi heard a rustling noise. It came from the forest.

"Shh!" she cautioned the girls. "Scoot closer to the fire. I heard something." She reached around the pine tree and curled her fingers around a thick branch. It wasn't much good against a real threat. A bear or a cougar would tear them apart.

But it might scare off a pesky coyote.

The girls huddled together. "What is it? A bear? A—"

"Just me."

Riley stepped into the firelight, gun drawn.

"Riley!" Andi threw the branch aside, leaped up, and flew into his arms. A sob caught in her throat.

Riley holstered his pistol and enfolded Andi in a heartfelt embrace. "Hey, it's all right. I'm here." He gently pulled her away and looked down at the others. "Is everyone all right?"

The two young ladies nodded.

"When we pulled up to the Wawona Hotel, I rented a horse and headed back. The others wanted to join me, but I could do what I needed to better alone." His looked turned grim.

Andi bit her lip. Riley had clearly planned on disarming—or killing if necessary—the two robbers. He meant business.

"My horse is tied about a hundred yards away. I slipped through the forest until I saw the fire. Then I waited. When I heard only you ladies, I assumed Troy and his cohort had left." He shook his head. "Which surprised me. The outlaw actually did what he said he'd do."

Riley sat down near the fire and drew Andi close.

"Well?" Amber wrinkled her forehead in confusion. "What are we waiting for? Let's be on our way."

"With one horse?" Riley chuckled. "No, ladies. We're here for the rest of the night. It's about midnight. I'll bring the horse back. You keep the fire going."

He winked at Andi. "I loaded the horse with plenty of supplies to make our first night camping pleasant—seeing as we're entertaining guests."

"But we can't stay here all night!" Martha wailed.

"I suppose you can walk if you really want to," Riley said pleasantly. "Follow the road straight up. It's an hour riding a horse, probably the rest of the night on foot."

Andi muffled a giggle when she saw the ladies' faces.

They slumped their acceptance.

When Riley left to bring back the horse and supplies, Andi gathered more firewood. It would be a long night.

Later, when their bellies were full of stew and hot coffee, the two city ladies curled up under their bedrolls.

Andi and Riley stayed up. She wasn't sleepy. Not in the least. She shared the reason she believed Troy had left them. Then she popped her surprise. She dropped the silver buckle and belt in Riley's lap.

His mouth fell open.

"I think Troy's had a change of heart," Andi said.

Riley raised his eyebrows, as if he didn't believe her.

She nodded. "It's true. He even made the other fellow leave all the loot behind."

Riley whistled softly. "Well, I'll be." He curled an arm around Andi's shoulders and drew her into his arms. "How's the honeymoon so far?" he asked, smiling.

Andi laughed. "The best ever. This adventure turned out better than I expected. I can't wait to see what happens next."

The rest of our honeymoon was not quite as adventurous as the way it began. Riley and I rented horses, loaded up camping supplies, and took off for the Yosemite Valley.

I planned on writing to Kate about Troy as soon as we returned home, but I forgot about it in the splendor of seeing my new house at Memory Creek ranch for the first time! The place was every bit as beautiful as I'd imagined, with lace curtains (Mother's handiwork) in each window, and even a china tea set of Aunt Rebecca's in the kitchen cabinet.

Riley didn't give me much time to look around, though. Grinning, he took my hand and led me to the barn, where he presented me with my wedding present—a brand-new saddle. With swirly etchings and lots of silver, it's even prettier than my birthday saddle from nine years ago! I squealed my joy and promptly slung the saddle over Shasta's back. "Let's go for a ride," I told Riley. He laughed at my enthusiasm and agreed.

House-touring and letter-writing could wait for a little while longer.

THE SHOOTING LESSON

MEMORY CREEK RANCH, CALIFORNIA, FALL 1886

Sometimes Riley can be as stubborn as Chad and the rest of the Carters. He got it into his head that it's time I finished learning how to shoot. Well, I know how to shoot. I just can't shoot straight.

Andi had plans for this beautiful October Saturday. She and Riley had just finished eating breakfast. From the paddock near the barn, Shasta whinnied.

"I'm coming!" she called. The pesky dishes could wait. A brisk ride was the only thing Andi could think of. A *long* ride.

Riley headed for the back door. "Are you going riding?"

Andi nodded. "Just as soon as I can manage it."

Riley paused when his hand grasped the doorknob. "I have something better in mind for this morning."

What was better than riding?

Andi looked suspiciously at her new husband. He was wearing an expression she was beginning to know well. "What?"

"I think it's about time you learned how to shoot."

Andi groaned. Riley couldn't be serious! "I can shoot."

His laugh sounded like a snort. "Not according to my sources."

That meant Riley had talked to that traitor of a brother, Chad. She let out a long, disgusted breath.

"You don't want to waste your morning trying to teach me to shoot a pistol, a rifle, or anything else that goes *bang*." She narrowed her eyes. "I'd prefer not to ruin my day . . . or yours."

Andi's poor shooting ability was the Carter family joke at her expense. *Not very funny, either.*

Chad had tried teaching her. It always ended in arguments and tears. Mitch had lent a hand once. That attempt had lasted ten minutes.

Justin was wise enough not to even try.

"It will be different with us," Riley argued. "I'm much more patient than Chad."

Andi couldn't disagree with that.

"I'm handy with a gun," Riley went on. "You need to learn how to handle a gun too. After all, sometimes you're here alone. I want you to get a varmint with the first shot."

Andi didn't reply. Shasta whinnied again. "I want to go riding." It came out as a childish whine.

"Let's do both," Riley suggested. "We'll ride up to the Banded Rocks and practice. You can pack a picnic lunch."

The Banded Rocks? That did sound like a good idea. She and Riley hadn't visited their special glade in months.

What's more, the look on Riley's face told Andi he wasn't going to take no for an answer.

She sighed. "Fine. This once."

"Swell!" A grin split Riley's face. "I'll saddle the horses."

He bounded out the door, leaving Andi to shake her head and wonder what she'd gotten herself into.

She winced. Shooting lessons had never turned out well for either Andi or the teacher.

She threw a lunch together, filled their canteens, slipped on her coat, and hurried outside. Might as well enjoy the ride. It would be a long one.

Riley had the horses ready. They tied their lunch and canteens to the horses' saddle horns and mounted up. Riley shoved his rifle into his scabbard, tightened his gun belt around his hips, and mounted.

Tucker yipped, begging to come along.

"Not this time, fella. Sorry."

Andi gave Riley a startled look. Tucker went everywhere with them. Was her husband so afraid she might miss and hit his beloved dog?

She opened her mouth to voice her accusation when it dawned on her that Tucker hadn't accompanied them to the Banded Rocks the last time they'd gone, either. She clamped her jaw shut and was silent.

Andi's spirits rose as they loped along the route to the Banded Rocks. She had a good two hours before she would be forced to think about pulling the trigger and humiliating herself. It had been three years since Chad's last—and final— attempt to teach her.

She wished it would be three more years before she had to try again. *Does Riley really think this lesson will end well?*

***

Riley pulled Dakota to a stop next to the scrawny pine Andi had learned to recognize as the marker near the secret entrance into their glade. When he dismounted and tied the appaloosa to a branch, Andi furrowed her forehead.

"We're not going into the glade to practice, are we?"

Riley shook his head. "I hadn't planned to. We don't want to startle the wildlife. It's better to practice out here in this barren wasteland. We'll have our picnic in the glade when we're finished."

"If we're still talking to each other by then," Andi muttered, dismounting.

"What did you say?"

She smiled. "Nothing important."

It was then Andi noticed the dusty burlap sack Riley had tied to his saddle. He loosened it, and the sack rattled.

"What's in there?"

Riley held up the sack. "The targets. I've been saving tin cans for just such a time as this."

Wonderful. Andi let out a long, resigned sigh. By the size of the bulge in the sack, he'd been planning this adventure for some time.

Riley cheerfully set to work finding a large, level rock the right distance away to begin the lesson. There were plenty of boulders to choose from, scattered all over the place and even into the narrow gap between the cliffs of the Banded Rocks.

Andi glanced wistfully toward the path to the glade. Then she straightened her shoulders and turned to her husband. "I'm ready."

Or not.

***

"We'll start simple," Riley said. He smiled and retraced his steps back to where Andi stood waiting.

"How simple?" she asked.

Riley held out his six-shooter.

Despite the cool autumn day, Andi's hands were sweaty as she gripped the handle.

"Easy-as-pie simple. The target is right over there." He pointed to the boulder. "You can practically spit and hit one of the cans."

This was not entirely true. The target's distance—near or far—did not matter so much to Andi. She would never hit it.

But she didn't want to tell Riley that. He would laugh and try to prove her wrong.

SUSAN K. MARLOW

Andi gritted her teeth, lifted the pistol, and pointed it at the can. A huge fist seemed to grab her throat, squeezing it until she could scarcely breathe. Her heart hammered against the inside of her chest.

Memories of other shooting lessons spun around in her mind. Chad huffing. Andi stomping and arguing. Then yelling and tears and—

I couldn't shoot straight then, she told herself. *I can't shoot straight now.* She swallowed past the lump in her throat. *I'm going to bungle this. Riley and I will get into a big fight.*

Andi lowered the pistol and set her jaw. *I won't shoot at all. Riley and I will eat our lunch and head back. He can't make me do this. It's too embarrassing.*

But then she looked at Riley. He was gazing at her, his eyes patient and encouraging. "Take your time, darling," he said. "There's no hurry. We have all day. Just give it your best shot."

This was very different from Chad's, *"For heaven's sake, Andi. How many times do I have to show you?"*

Her resolve melted like butter on a hot summer's day.

He thinks I can do it. Andi squirmed. *I can't let him down! I can't let him think his wife is a quitter. A Carter never quits. Neither does a Prescott.*

Another thought elbowed its way in. *I'll give it my best shot, like he told me to do.* She grinned. "Thanks, Riley."

And when she did make a perfect shot, she would show Chad just how good his baby sister was with a gun! *So there!*

Just like that, her anxiety slipped away like water off a duck's back. She lifted the pistol and pulled the trigger.

Bang!

Andi stumbled backward. She missed the can. She missed the boulder.

Her spirits crumpled.

Riley came up beside her. "Before you try it again, here's what I want you to do."

Slowly and patiently he reminded her to hold the pistol with both hands for more stability. He sighted along her outstretched arms and nodded. "You've got it in your sights."

As if that would do any good.

"Spread your legs a bit, so you can keep your balance. You felt the pistol's kickback when the first shot went off."

Andi reddened. She'd forgotten about that. *Well, three years is a long time.*

"Now," Riley went on, "take a deep breath and hold it."

Andi looked at him. "What? Why?"

Chad had never told her to hold her breath. It was "point and shoot" with big brother. And be quick about it. You never knew when a varmint might sneak up on you.

Riley's idea sounded silly. Chad was right. You had to be quick!

"Just try it," Riley suggested. "It can't hurt."

Point taken. Andi sucked in her breath and held it.

"Good," Riley encouraged. "Now breathe out, and *slowly* pull the trigger. Don't jerk it."

Andi did what he said.

Zing! The bullet hit the can.

Andi whooped. "I did it, Riley! I really and truly hit that can. And on the first try too." *Well, the second try today, but who's counting?*

"Whoa there." He took the pistol. "Don't swing it around like a lasso."

Andi's cheeks heated. She knew better than that. Chad would have bawled her out good and plenty for being so careless around a firearm.

When the pistol was safely in Riley's hands, he smiled.

"I knew you could do it." He gave Andi's long, thick braid a gentle tug.

Andi laughed. "I've never heard of anybody taking a breath and holding it before they shoot. Not Mitch, or Justin, or Chad. Not even Mother."

Riley nodded. "I thought it was a ridiculous notion too, when my pa started teaching me to shoot. But when you're first learning, it helps to steady and calm you, and you have a better chance at a good shot."

That made sense. Then she frowned. "Why didn't Chad ever think of telling me to take a deep breath? He should have taken a breath or two also. It would have kept us both a lot calmer."

Riley shrugged. "He probably forgot that aspect of a beginning shooter. Once you become a crack shot, you don't need to take that breath. You'll just point and shoot, like Chad or Mitch." He grinned. "And like me."

Andi gave Riley a shove. "Let me try it again—just in case that first shot was beginner's luck." Confidence surged through her.

But her confidence made Andi too sure of herself.

Fifteen minutes later, her stomach turned over with frustration. Her cheeks flamed. Her coat had been flung to the ground and sweat poured down her neck in rivulets.

Every one of her shots had hit the boulder, the ground, the twisted manzanita bush, or the sky. Not another can fell. No satisfying *zing*.

Wouldn't Chad laugh at that! Andi could hear him now. *"I told you so, Riley. She's hopeless."* Never! Her hands shook.

"You're wound up tighter than a top," Riley said. "You need to calm down."

"No, I'm not," Andi argued through clenched teeth.

Bang! The shot ricocheted off the boulder and into the dust.

"Andi!" Riley jumped back. "Take it easy."

Her frustration boiled over, spilling out in hot tears and angry words. "I'm tired of doing this!" she wailed. "I'm tired of this lesson! I told you I'm no good with a gun!"

Andi sat down and flung the pistol away. The years rolled back. Next, Chad would yank her up and holler at her for not taking care of the firearm. He'd send her back to the house.

"Andi!" Riley sat down and engulfed her in a warm embrace. "Shh. It's all right. You're tired, and you gave it your best shot. We can try it again another time. Let's head for the glade and eat our lunch."

Andi's breath caught at the end of a sob. For an instant she felt disoriented.

Chad? No! It was Riley, calming her with gentle words. She blinked back her tears.

"I'm sorry if I ruined your day," Riley said softly. "Let's not let any silly shooting lesson come between us." He squeezed her and planted a kiss on her cheek.

Andi returned to the here and now. Shame replaced frustration. "I'm sorry I lost my temper. For one horrible moment I thought I was fifteen years old again, and back at the ranch."

She smiled through watery eyes. "Chad never hugged me or told me I gave it my best shot." She shrugged. "Of course, I never gave him a chance to be nice to me. I usually ran off crying. One time, I even threw the pistol at the target."

"You didn't!"

Andi nodded. "I did. I almost hit it too. Chad blew up. He went on a rant about the danger, not to mention it was his favorite pearl-handled Colt."

She winced at the memory. "That was my final shooting lesson with big brother. He yelled at me as I ran to the house, 'We're done with this for good! You're never touching my pistol again!' And I shouted back, 'Fine by me!'"

"No wonder Chad blew up." Riley shook his head. "You shouldn't have done that."

"I know. I apologized later, but he and I were glad there would be no more lessons." Andi leaned back into Riley's strong arms and glanced up into his face. "At least I got one good shot off this morning." She grinned. "It's a start."

He smiled back. "It was perfect. "Let's sneak into the glade and have our picnic lunch," Riley said. "I'm starved."

Andi rose. She brushed off her split skirt and found Riley's pistol. "You know what? I think I should take one more shot. I've calmed down and feel ready to prove that first shot wasn't a fluke. What do you think?"

Riley gave her a two-fingered salute from the brim of his hat. "You go right ahead, my dear. I'll check the horses and grab our lunch. You might be happier without an audience."

When Riley had disappeared around one of the larger boulders, Andi made her way to the tin cans. Two had tipped over in the breeze. They lay on their sides on top of the boulder. Another can had dropped and lay on the ground.

Humming, Andi straightened two of the cans. Then she reached down to pick up the last one.

Bzzz. Andi froze, her hand halfway to the ground. Not six feet away, a large rattlesnake lay coiled. Clearly, it had awakened from a mid-morning snooze between the boulders and had decided to come out for a sunbath.

Bzzz. The snake's rattle shook vigorously. Its head rose, and its tongue flashed in and out.

Andi's throat went dry. If only Riley was here!

She knew as long as she stayed still, the snake wouldn't strike. How long could she wait? For Riley's return?

Riley wouldn't know to bring the rifle back, and he didn't have the pistol. She did.

Andi tightened her grip around the handle of the Colt .44. Inch by inch, she brought it up to face the snake.

Both hands on the pistol. *Yes. Take a breath and hold it.* She did. She willed her hands not to shake.

Bang! The gun went off. *Bang!* Two shots. Then a final shot. *Bang!*

When Andi realized the snake was dead, she slumped to the ground.

Riley rounded the boulder just then. "The horses are fine. I heard three shots. Did you hit any of the cans?"

Andi turned to face him. "I didn't hit *any* of them," she whispered. "I got *that.*" She swallowed and pointed to the limp rattlesnake. Her hand shook.

Riley's mouth fell open. He found a stick and hurried to the snake. Two pokes later, he looked at her. "All three shots hit it," he said in wonder.

Andi set the pistol down and stood. A tiny blaze of joy started in her belly. It spread quickly to engulf her whole body. "I shot the rattlesnake! I didn't miss."

Riley pulled Andi into his arms and kissed her. "You sure do beat all, my courageous little wife. You can't hit a tin can, but who cares?" He started laughing. "You shot something much more dangerous. I'd say today's lesson is a rousing success."

Andi knew she needed a few more lessons. She wanted to give the rifle a try.

But for now? Well, she felt mighty pleased with herself.

Wait 'til Chad hears about this!

RATTLESNAKE STEW

MEMORY CREEK RANCH, CALIFORNIA, FALL 1886

Perhaps someday I will be glad I recorded this event in my journal. We might all laugh over it. Or maybe not. Alas, as Proverbs says, "Pride goeth before destruction, and a haughty spirit before a fall." I had pride. I fell. And I almost took my sister-in-law Ellie with me.

Andi couldn't help feeling smug. Her recent shooting lesson with Riley had turned out better than she ever imagined.

She'd killed a rattlesnake during her first shooting practice in over three years. Wait until the family heard about this!

She didn't even blink when Riley suggested they take the snake home. Maybe he wanted to parade it in front of his boss, Chad. His new brother-in-law had succeeded where Chad had failed.

Andi could shoot, after all.

Reality hit a day later. Riley did not want to show off the snake to the rest of the Carter family. At least, not in the way Andi assumed.

"Ever had rattlesnake stew?" he asked innocently.

Andi nodded. "It tastes a little bit like chicken. It's all right, so long as you put enough other stuff in the pot to hide the fact that it's a rattlesnake."

She made a face. *Not my favorite meal.*

"What better way to show Chad you can shoot than to invite him over for rattlesnake stew." Riley chuckled. "From the snake *you* shot."

Riley had a strange sense of humor sometimes.

"What do you say?" he urged.

"I suppose . . ." Andi's words trailed off when a new thought came to mind. Riley was right. It might be fun. "All right," she said. "I'll do it."

"Great! I'll ride over and invite Chad and Ellie for supper tonight." He kissed Andi good-bye and bounded out of the house.

Andi peeked at the huge reptile lying coiled in the dishpan. Just because she'd eaten rattlesnake as a child didn't mean she wanted to cook one.

Then she put her hands on her hips. She'd watched Cook prepare rattlesnake stew for the hands more than once. How hard could it be?

Baking wasn't Andi's best skill, but stew had never failed her. It would be easy to substitute rattlesnake meat for the beef.

Andi would probably not see Riley for the rest of the day. He was working for Chad today, which made it convenient to bring his boss and Ellie to Memory Creek after work.

"Better get to it," Andi said aloud. She transferred the reptile from the sink to the large worktable in the middle of the kitchen.

Under Andi's sharp knife, the head sliced off. *Whack!* The tail came next. She held up the rattles and counted each one. There were ten, which meant it was a big snake.

"Plenty of meat for the stew pot," Andi said happily.

So far, so good.

Andi switched to her long, thin skinning knife.

It sliced through the rattlesnake's underbelly slicker than a knife through butter. She peeled the edges back.

"Ugh!" Andi jumped back. Her stomach turned over.

Two partially digested mice stared up at her. Andi gagged and quickly got rid of them. Then she scrubbed her hands under the kitchen pump before continuing.

Thankfully, there were no other signs of recently eaten meals inside the snake's belly. It was slimy, but once the mice were gone, the snake rinsed easily.

Let's see. What next? Andi furrowed her brow and tried to visualize Cook at work, quickly cleaning, dicing, and cooking up a rattlesnake.

The skin!

She couldn't cook the snake with its skin on. Andi took a firm hold of one end of the long reptile and started pulling. To her surprise, it slipped off much easier than she expected.

That's when the first pinch of pride sneaked in.

"I killed this snake on the first shot, and now we're going to eat it," Andi told Tucker, who had pawed open the back door and sat on his haunches nearby. His tail wagged.

For once, Riley had told his dog to stick close to home instead of following his master everywhere he went. Andi liked having Tucker to talk to.

"Very wilderness of me," Andi went on. "I bet I could survive out there with just a knife and a pistol. I would never starve." She giggled. "No sirree!"

Tucker lay down and put his head on his front paws.

"I'll make sure you get your share, fella," Andi said.

Once she had the snake skinned and thoroughly rinsed, she lowered the whole thing into a pot of boiling water. "Two hours should do it," she said. "That should make the meat simply fall off the bones."

While the snake boiled, Andi searched the bins for a fresh lemon. Cook always said a lemon took away the gamey flavor of wild creatures. "I'd rather the stew tasted like bland rabbit or chicken than bland snake."

When she found a lemon, she sliced it in half and tossed both halves into the pot.

The snake boiled for a full two hours. Andi sniffed. The lemon really did help. A mild odor wafted up in the steam. Only a faint trace of rattlesnake filled her nostrils.

Andi set the pot aside when it had fully cooked. She let it cool before checking it. Most of the water had boiled away. She kept what water was left for the stew.

Using a slotted spoon, she lifted the snake from the pot. The meat fell away from dozens of small, soft bones.

Andi's pride ballooned. Not one thing had gone wrong. *Maybe I should enter this dish in the State Fair.*

The cooling snake lay in pieces on the worktable. Andi picked through it in record time. She tossed the tiny bones aside and cut the stringy snake meat into pieces. Then she returned the meat to the stew pot.

Next came the vegetables. She cut up potatoes, onions, and tomatoes and added them to the pot. She sprinkled in a generous amount of salt, pepper, parsley, basil, and even poured in some beef broth she found in the icebox.

Now it really smelled good! Andi's pride knew no bounds.

By the time Riley, Chad, and Ellie rode up to the ranch house, the kitchen smelled wonderful—like spices, not like rattlesnake. Andi couldn't wait to show off her rattlesnake stew and share her I'm-a-good-shot-now story with Chad.

Andi dipped a spoon into the thick concoction, blew on it, and took a taste. Wonder of wonders! This stew tasted good, even by Mother's standards.

She turned to Tucker just before Riley and his guests entered. "Who would have thought that rattlesnake stew would be one of my first major cooking successes?"

Tucker's tail thumped against the floorboards. When the back door opened, he scurried outside.

Riley entered the kitchen. He sniffed and raised his eyebrows. "Supper smells delicious."

His words warmed Andi's heart.

"I need to change before we eat," he announced and ducked into the bedroom.

Chad and Ellie climbed the steps. "Knock, knock!"

Andi pushed open the screen door. "Come on in."

Chad had changed out of his ranch clothes before driving over. *Probably Ellie's doing,* Andi thought. He looked fresh and clean-shaven.

Ellie, as always, looked lovely, even being in the family way. Andi could hardly tell Ellie was carrying her first baby. She was clever with a needle, and her dresses covered her growing belly as nicely as Andi had ever see it done.

She tucked away this knowledge for the future. Ellie might be able to do wonders to alter Andi's dresses. She smiled dreamily.

I can't wait to hold my own baby someday.

The smell of baking biscuits jerked Andi back to the present. She didn't want them to burn. She hurried to the huge cast-iron cook stove and opened the door.

Perfect!

"What's this I hear about you shooting a rattler?" Chad started right in.

Andi shot a surprised look at Riley. "You told him."

Riley shrugged. "I couldn't help it," he apologized. "It just came out. I was just so pleased and proud."

Chad shook his head. "And Riley wasn't there to keep you from shooting your foot?"

Very funny. Andi was bursting with her own measure of pride, though, so she ignored his teasing. "One shot, big brother. *Bang!* I got it. Then I put two more rounds into that varmint to make sure he was good and dead."

She smiled up at him. "I'm a crack shot now."

"Good for you," he said, like he really meant it.

Andi beamed. She set the pot of stew and the biscuits in the middle of the table. "Let's eat."

Chad held the chair for Ellie then sat down. He dropped his napkin on his lap and peered into the stew pot. "Riley told me we're having stew tonight." His lip twisted. "It's . . . well, it's all right to eat, isn't it? Not burnt or anything?"

Andi rolled her eyes. Her reputation as a lousy cook had spread far and wide.

"For heaven's sake, Chad," Ellie scolded. "Leave her alone." She smiled at Andi. "It smells heavenly. What kind of stew is it?"

"Rattlesnake," Andi answered, taking her place.

Chad's eyes bugged out. "The one you shot?"

"Of course," Andi bantered back. "Where would I get another one?" For once she didn't have to worry about the meal. She already knew it tasted good.

Everybody paused while Riley asked the blessing, then Chad dished himself a bowl of stew. He took a tiny taste and chewed. So did Riley.

Chad's eyes lit up. "Not bad, little sister." He dug in for another spoonful.

Riley grinned. "Not bad? Why, this is delicious."

Ellie scooped up a heaping spoonful. "I've always liked rattlesnake. Sometimes it's all we had to eat."

She put a bite in her mouth, chewed, and swallowed. "Pa was better at finding snakes than he was at finding gold. This is better than any rattlesnake Pa fixed back in Goldtown."

Andi should have said "thank you" and humbly changed the subject. She could have asked Ellie about baby names or baby clothes or anything that might be useful someday if God blessed her and Riley with a little one.

Instead, Andi talked non-stop about how she had shot that snake and skinned it. She had the sense to leave the half-eaten mice out of her recital, but she included everything else. Especially how easy it was, and how the meat had slipped so effortlessly from all those tiny bones.

She was chattering like a magpie when Ellie's face suddenly turned red. Andi's sister-in-law dropped her spoon and pushed back her chair.

"What's wrong?" Andi jumped up from her seat. "Is the baby all right?" Carrying a child could sometimes be a risky venture. "Are *you* all right?"

Ellie shook her head and pointed to her mouth. No words came out. Not even a peep.

She was obviously *not* all right. Andi's breath caught. What could be wrong?

"Did you burn your tongue?" Riley asked. "Or bite it?"

"What's the matter, sweetheart?" Chad asked.

Ellie's face grew redder. She looked desperate.

Riley's eyes widened. "Something's caught in her throat!"

Ellie's eyes rolled back. She couldn't get any air.

Andi's heart plunged to her toes. *Dear God, don't let her die! Don't let her unborn baby die!*

Chad leaped into action. For all his brash ways, Andi's brother was a quick thinker. He grabbed his wife and nearly turned her upside down.

Andi wasn't sure how Chad did it—things happened too fast—but suddenly a small clump of fine bones spewed from Ellie's mouth.

She choked and took three big breaths. Then she slumped in Chad's arms. He settled her back in her chair.

Andi felt faint. Rattlesnake bones? *Oh please, no!* But the truth could not be covered up. *I almost killed my sister-in-law.* She could have died so quickly.

Andi kicked herself mentally. She had been cocky this afternoon, thinking how clever she was the whole time she'd been skinning, cooking, and deboning the snake.

She didn't say a word. She couldn't. An apology seemed worthless. She glanced at Chad. Would her brother ever forgive her? She sat down in her chair, covered her face, and bawled.

The next minute Riley had Andi in his arms. "It's all right," he crooned. "All's well that ends well."

Andi didn't need her mother's favorite saying right then. Her head was full of what-ifs. Over and over, Andi saw Ellie lying still and lifeless on her kitchen floor, with soft rattlesnake bones lodged in her throat.

Andi's heart didn't return to normal until Chad and Ellie both insisted everything was all right.

"These things happen," Ellie explained. "It's really my own fault. If I'd been eating like a lady with small bites, I would have felt the bones in my mouth before I swallowed them." She laughed. "Like usual, though, I was wolfing down that delicious stew. It's no wonder I missed a bone or two."

Even Chad smiled. "Leave it to you, Andi. Life is never dull with you around."

Riley gave Andi a warm hug and planted a kiss on her forehead. "That's for sure!"

109

EIGHT

SIERRA ADVENTURE

MEMORY CREEK RANCH, CALIFORNIA, DECEMBER 1886

There is nothing I would like more this first Christmas on our new ranch than to continue the Circle C family tradition of going up to the high country and choosing a tree. The problem will be convincing Riley that he should be part of this tradition.

Chapter 1

Every year since eighteen-year-old Andrea Carter Prescott could remember, the Christmas holidays always began with her three big brothers going up into the Sierras to cut down the family tree.

When she was very small, Andi waited all day long—her freckled nose pushed up against the window pane—to see what kind of tree they would bring home.

In those early days, Father went along with the boys. When he returned, all smiles, he would toss Andi up in the air. "Andrea, just see what your brothers and I brought home *this* year. A very tall tree, and thick enough for you to climb!"

But Father never let Andi climb it. He and Mother also never let her have anything to do with the candles, which shone bright and cheery from every other branch.

"They are too dangerous," Mother always warned. "Keep away from them. You don't want to burn down the house."

Andi always obeyed that restriction.

Later, after Father died, the boys kept up the tradition. When Andi was nine years old, Justin, Chad, and Mitch let her go along. Melinda was away at school in San Francisco, and besides, her sister was never eager to join in with any tree-cutting expeditions.

Andi found out why soon enough. An unexpected blizzard during her first Christmas-tree trek into the mountains sent Andi and her brothers hiding out all night under the wagon. The icy wind and snow whipped around them. It was a scary sound, and she was so cold!

After that, Andi decided she would wait until she was much, *much* older to go with them again. It was more fun—and warmer—to meet the boys at the door and help decorate the Douglas or red fir than to freeze half to death.

Andi was telling Riley all about the Circle C holiday tradition one evening in early December. They sat out on the front porch and watched the sun go down in a blaze of color.

Andi wore a light sweater, and Riley a flannel shirt. The hills had not yet seen the onset of rain and mud. Just sunny days and cool, crisp nights.

Perfect weather for working. But not perfect weather for getting into the Christmas spirit.

"I thought it might be fun to start the same tradition in our own family," Andi ventured.

Riley gave her an unenthusiastic look. "I bet I can find a nice tree at a spot much lower in elevation. Why go clear to the snowline?" He didn't have a high opinion of snow and cold.

Andi's heart sank. "It won't be the same."

How could she explain? Andi loved being married to Riley—they were best friends—but she was beginning to feel she would miss out on her favorite Circle C tradition.

SUSAN K. MARLOW

"I think your tradition is on its way out," Riley said. "Your brothers don't have time anymore to tear themselves away and cut down trees. Justin lives in town with two lively little kids." He smiled. "I doubt Ellie will let Chad go so far up into the mountains on his own, especially with her being in the family way and so close to her time."

Andi winced. Too true.

Riley chuckled. "And Mitch? Ha! He's in town more often than he's on the ranch, according to the big boss."

Andi narrowed her eyes. What had Chad been telling Riley lately? With their own Memory Creek ranch winding down on work for the season, Riley had spent the last few weeks working for Chad.

Had Mitch finally found a likely young lady to court? If so, he sure hadn't told Andi about it.

Even if he had found someone, Andi was certain none of her family wanted to do away with such a special tradition. Why, just a year ago—before Andi married—she and Mitch and Chad had done the honors of bringing home the tree.

Riley had volunteered to stay home and boss the ranch.

"Maybe you and Chad can go," she suggested sweetly. "You could get three trees—or maybe four. One for the ranch house, one for our place, and one for Justin and Lucy. I bet Melinda and Peter would appreciate a little fir or spruce for their place in town too."

Riley mumbled something that sounded like, "I'm not a tree merchant. Let Peter get his own tree."

"All right then. Peter can look out for Melinda's tree. But what about this?" She took a deep breath and let the words fly out. "I could come along with you and Chad. We wouldn't even need a wagon. Three horses. Three trees. Just pull them behind the horses."

112

Riley laughed and stood up from the porch swing. "You can't be serious."

"Never more."

Riley craned his neck and glanced toward the majestic Sierra Nevada range. "The snowline is awfully high this year," he said. "I'm not a mountain climber, and neither is Dakota."

He looked at Andi. "Dragging trees behind the horses over dry ground will ruin them. I think you know that."

Andi stood up and joined him. "Not all the way to the snowline then. But I won't have a scraggly pine tree—and neither will anybody else in the family. Could we just go high enough to find a nice fir? We could take the wagon."

Riley scratched his chin. "Well . . ."

Andi could tell he was weakening. "Please?"

He smiled. "I reckon it's not the end of the world if I take a day off and cut down a Christmas tree, if it means that much to you."

"It does!" Andi threw her arms around Riley and kissed his cheek. "I can go along, right?"

"Of course." Riley hugged her. "Why don't you and I go by ourselves and surprise the rest of your family? I'm pretty sure Chad won't be budged from Ellie's side."

He whispered, "Family traditions *are* important. Sorry for being a killjoy at first."

Andi squealed. "When shall we go?"

Riley waved an arm toward the west. "Red sky tonight, sailors' delight," he quoted. "Looks like it will be a sunny day tomorrow. Let's take the day off and just get it done."

Andi tore Riley's wide-brimmed hat from his head and threw it up in the air. "Yee-haw!"

"You can't seem to shake that little-girl enthusiasm from your soul, can you?" Riley teased.

"I don't intend too," Andi replied saucily. "No sirree! Not if I live to be eighty years old and have a dozen kids and dozens of grandchildren."

Riley winked. "I wouldn't have it any other way."

Chapter 2

SIERRA HIGH COUNTRY, CALIFORNIA, DECEMBER 1886

*H*urry, hurry! Andi told herself the next morning. *Before Riley changes his mind and goes off on his own.* It was one thing to have the softly setting sun move Riley to agree to let Andi go along on an all-day trek into the high country.

It was an entirely different matter to look at it in the clean air of a new day.

If he knew my secret, he would never let me go along on this adventure. A twinge of guilt for keeping something so important from Riley tweaked Andi's conscience, but she brushed it off.

After all, Andi had accompanied her brothers a number of times since she'd grown up. It was not a dangerous journey. Just a long day. And often a long hike on snowshoes when they were forced to abandon the wagon and horses not far above the snowline.

But today was perfect. The snowline was so high this year that she and Riley could take the wagon all the way to where the best trees grew.

Andi giggled as she packed a good supply of food, coffee, and blankets. "We can probably back the wagon right up to the trees of our choice, cut them down, and let each one drop into the wagon bed."

Her spirits rose high as a circling hawk. This would be the most fun ever! Just she and Riley, an ax and a saw, a picnic lunch, and a couple of horses. Oh yes, and a dog.

She twirled in a quick circle and suddenly felt dizzy. Her arms splayed out. She caught herself just in time on the edge of the table.

Settle down, girl, she warned herself.

A good knock on the head if she tripped and fell during her silly twirls would keep her home for sure. She smoothed back the stray waves that had escaped from her long, dark braid. She untied her apron and hung it up just as Riley bounded inside through the back door.

The screen door slammed shut behind him. "The wagon's hitched up." He groaned when he picked up the heavy baskets. "This is an all-day outing, not a weekend camping trip. What's in here?"

"Enough grub to keep us going so I don't have to fix supper tonight after we stagger back, exhausted, from our tree-cutting expedition." She gave Riley a shove toward the door. "I'll be too tired."

It took a few more minutes to collect warm coats, hats, and blankets and settle their supplies in the back of the wagon. It might not be snowing or blizzard conditions in the mountains, but it would be chilly the beginning of December.

From experience, Andi knew it was best to be prepared when one ventured into the high country.

"Let's go!" Riley boosted Andi up onto the high wagon seat and climbed up beside her. He jiggled the reins. "Giddup, Ranger. C'mon, Buster."

Then he gave a shrill whistle. A small black and white collie-type dog tore around the barn, barking excitedly.

"In you go, Tucker."

Riley snapped his fingers, and Tucker leaped into the back of the wagon. His tail swished.

The two horses—one black, one white—whinnied their enthusiasm and broke into a lively trot.

Andi and Riley's Memory Creek ranch lay much closer to the Sierras than the Circle C ranch house—a whole hour closer. In no time, it seemed, the horses had carried them up higher and higher into the hills.

Riley pushed his wide-brimmed hat farther down on his forehead. Andi followed suit with her own hat. The morning sun had risen and shone right in their eyes. True to the "sailor's delight" saying, the day was clear and sunny.

Andi felt like singing, but a little bug of disappointment pinched her thoughts. "Dashing through the snow in a one-horse open sleigh" didn't quite ring true on a morning that seemed like a crisp fall day. "Jingle Bells" sounded better while driving through a few inches of snow.

She sighed. No snow today.

The important thing, though, was that she and Riley were bringing home a tree . . . or two or three. Mother would be thrilled. Chad would be relieved that he could stay near Ellie right now, and of course Justin and Lucy would be grateful.

As for Mitch, if what Chad had told Riley was true, Mitch probably wasn't thinking about Christmas or holiday traditions. He was too caught up with courting.

Hmmm, I wonder who it could be? Emily McConnell? Sarah Mead?

Andi spent a few more minutes thinking about who might be a potential new sister-in-law. Then her thoughts turned to how much fun it would be to watch Sammy and little Gracie jump for joy when they saw the tree Aunt Andi and Uncle Riley would bring their folks.

She smiled. Someday in the not-too-distant future . . .

Andi shook her head to clear her thoughts. "So, Riley," she said suddenly. "What did you and your folks used to do for Christmas? Was your tree big? Small? Did you see your grandparents or aunts or uncles? The only relative *we* ever saw at Christmas was Aunt Rebecca, and most of the time I was not happy about that."

Riley shook the reins to encourage the horses to get a move-on and didn't answer. The far-off look in his eyes told Andi she had stumbled on a sore spot.

Christmas would not be the happiest of memories for Riley as a little boy. He'd spent three years on the Circle C as a child. The one year he was giddy with excitement when he learned that he might go home to San Francisco had come crashing down at the last moment.

Finally, Riley said, "The merriest Christmas I ever spent was when I was eight. It was at your place, when Uncle Sid surprised me by fetching my mother and bringing her to the ranch."

A smile spread across his face at the memory. "She felt so much better. Don't you remember? She stayed two whole months! What a wonderful Christmas present that was for me."

Andi nodded and squeezed Riley's arm. "I remember. Your mother and mine got along wonderfully well. It was too bad when she had to go back to the city. She wasn't strong enough to care for you, and your father sure was gone a lot. So, you had to stay on the ranch."

She grinned. "I have to say that I'm glad you stayed."

"I am too." Riley shrugged. "The rest of my Christmases after I left the Circle C were off and on, kind of haphazard, what with the Army transferring Pa all over the West."

He gave Andi a crooked smile. "A cactus does *not* make a very good Christmas tree. One Christmas at Fort Yuma I tried to use one. Bad mistake. I was so poked and bleeding by the time I hauled the cactus home that Mama had to bandage me up and down both arms."

Andi burst out laughing. "You never told me that!"

Riley was laughing now too. "I reckon there are some stories that seem awful when you're going through them, but they're sort of funny now."

He lost his smile. "Nothing about Fort Alcatraz has good memories, though, especially not any Christmases. What a rainy, dreary prison duty *that* was for my family." He shuddered.

"Well," Andi told him firmly. "This is our first Christmas together. I'm bound and determined to make it the best Christmas ever for both of us. You just see if I don't."

Riley tipped his hat at her. "Yes, *ma'am*."

Chapter 3

I love the high country. The air is always so fresh, clean, and crispy cold, even when the sun is shining. The trees grow straight and tall—Douglas fir, red fire, even Jeffrey pine, with its vanilla-smelling bark. Mmmm! I could stay up here all afternoon.

It was barely noon when Riley pulled the wagon to a stop near a likely stand of trees. "What do you think about these?"

Andi jerked her head up. She'd been dozing off and on the last half hour. "Huh? What?"

"You all right?" Riley asked, squinting down at her.

"Oh, sure. It's just that the last few miles of any trip wears a body down. I'm cramped and tired of sitting on this hard seat. What did you ask me?"

Riley waved his arm toward the trees. "Do any of these firs strike your fancy?"

Andi studied the stand. White fir, with a sprinkling of Douglas fir, grew at varying heights. These trees looked all right, but a white-tipped red fir was more to her liking.

They would have to go much higher than this to find a solid stand of red fir. They grew above 5,000 feet, and already the horses looked winded from the climb. Andi shaded her eyes. And was that snow up there? Probably.

And I'm so tired!

"Yes, a couple of these white fir should do just fine," she decided. "So long as you can find at least one of them ten feet tall for the ranch house. The parlor there has a higher ceiling than either Justin's place or our sitting room." She gave him a challenging look.

"Let's go then." Riley jumped down from the wagon seat. "*You* are going to pick out these trees, my dear. I'll cut them down." He gave Andi a hand to the ground. "You're the experienced Carter Christmas tree lady, after all."

The two of them tramped through the forest, chatting and laughing. Tucker raced back and forth, tail wagging.

Andi couldn't decide which tree she liked best. One looked tall enough, but some of the branches near the top were dead and bare. Another showed deer damage smack in the center of the tree.

Still another had a crooked trunk. Two more looked tall enough for her own home, but either one would look puny in Mother's parlor.

"Hmm," Andi pondered. "It's hard to decide."

"They all look alike to me." Riley leaned against the trunk of a huge Ponderosa pine. He whacked the grooved, orange-colored bark and winked. "Should I chop this one down?"

Andi didn't rise to his joke. "I told you, no pines. Besides, even you can tell this one's a giant." She walked another fifty yards.

Sighing, Riley followed.

Another half hour passed. Andi felt like they were going around in circles. Then she saw it. "Over here, Riley! It's perfect in every way."

Riley hurried over. He whistled softly. "It certainly is."

The white fir stood tall and proud, perfectly symmetrical, with not one flaw. It soared a good ten feet above their heads. The trunk near the ground was probably eight inches across.

"You really know how to pick 'em," Riley admitted. "It's a beauty." He removed his coat, slipped his gloves on, and tightened his grip on the ax. "I'll get started on this one. It just needs a little undercut, and then I'll use the saw. You go back to the wagon and coax the horses here. I've no desire to drag this tree any distance."

"If we both pull, we could haul it back."

"No, it's too much work when the wagon can easily be moved." Riley pointed through the trees. "I see it way over yonder. There's enough clearing between the stands. You should have no problem weaving your way over here."

Andi agreed and started back. "Come on, Tucker."

Tucker's ears pricked up. He looked from Andi to Riley and gave a little bark.

"Oh, all right," Andi gave in. "Stay with Riley. Don't let him chop of his leg, y'hear?"

Tucker wagged his tail.

"And mark any other likely trees on your way," Riley called after her.

Andi waved and kept going. She plodded through the forest, keeping her eye on the way they'd come. It took longer than she thought it would.

I'm so tired, Andi thought when she saw the wagon with its pile of blankets heaped in the bed. The sun shone down, warm and pleasant. *What a cozy place for a nap.*

Andi knew better than to take a rest. She heard the biting chops of Riley's ax then the back-and-forth sound of sawing. He needed the wagon, so she hurried to do what he asked. Wearily, she climbed up on the wooden seat and gathered up the reins.

"Giddup, boys," she ordered the horses.

Slowly and carefully, Andi weaved her way around various stands of trees. The horses seemed skittish for some reason. Ranger shook his mane and whinnied. Buster pinned back his ears.

"For goodness' sake, fellas. It's just Riley chopping down a tree. He's made louder noises than that back on the ranch."

But the horses did not settle down.

Andi urged them on, following the sound of Riley's ax. She had to drive them in a roundabout way to avoid forest trash and clumps of young trees growing close together.

Andi was a good driver. She kept Ranger and Buster on a tight rein and ordered them again to settle down.

"I know it's tight in some places but—"

Sudden loud barking—desperate barking—sent a sliver of fear through Andi's heart. She also heard a strange, eerily familiar sound.

The horses stopped short and refused to go a step farther.

More loud barking. And growling.

121

Ranger's front legs rose. He strained against the harness and snorted before slamming his front feet down. Buster whinnied. He sounded frightened. Luckily, the clearing was too narrow to allow the horses to bolt. If they'd been on the range, however, the horses would be a couple of runaways right now.

Why? Andi shivered. "Riley?" she called.

Instead of his cheerful "I'm over here!" a low scream filled Andi's ears. A moaning, growling scream. Uncontrollable barking erupted from Tucker.

Andi's stomach turned over in horror. *Oh please, God, no! Not now. Not here.*

Chapter 4

The horses had known all along.

Tucker was also proclaiming loud and clear that a mountain lion prowled nearby. It had probably seen Riley. For sure it saw Tucker. But surely the cat wouldn't stalk a man! Normally, the tawny-colored beasts were skittish and kept far away from humans.

Well, it's here now!

Andi whirled. Her gaze flew to the rifle that lay on the bottom of the wagon bed. She leaped over the seat and landed in the back of the wagon. Her shaking fingers curled around the warm iron barrel, where it had soaked up the sun.

Thank you, God, that Riley never goes anywhere without his rifle!

Clutching the rifle to her chest, Andi scrambled over the wagon side and dropped to the ground. Then she took a deep breath and staggered to her feet.

"Riley!" Her words came out as a choked cry.

She heard a low snarl. Tucker wouldn't stop barking.

Andi's heart raced. "Riley!" This time it was a shriek.

"Tucker, back!" Riley's voice sounded far away. "Stay away. Don't come near!"

Part of Andi's numbed mind tried to figure out her husband's command. Was he yelling at Tucker or at her? The other part of her mind screamed, *Riley has only a small dog and an ax. An ax against a cougar. I have the rifle.*

Fear for Riley's life made Andi's feet fly through the woods. Then she stopped short.

There was no need to shoot the cat. Just firing the rifle would most likely scare it off. It had scared away another cougar all those years ago, when she'd shot a rifle through the window of a mountain shack.

At the thought, Andi didn't delay. *Crack! Crack!* She fired two shots into the air. *Crack!* She fired one more for good measure.

It must have run off at the rifle shots. Andi ran as fast as she could. Her breath came in small gasps. "Riley!"

She tore around a clump of dogwood and black oak and came face to face with Riley and Tucker . . . and the cat.

Impossible!

The rifle shots had not frightened the cougar. It stood crouching, snarling at Riley, who was waving an ax back and forth and yelling.

Tucker rushed at the cougar, then leaped out of the way at the swipe of a huge paw. He circled the mountain lion, growling, barking, protecting Riley.

Why doesn't the cat run away?

Andi's drumming heart pounded in her ears. Her stomach heaved.

"Shoot it!" Riley's voice cracked. His face was white.

Andi wasn't sure she could hit the cougar. She'd been practicing this fall, but her aim was not consistent. What if she shot Tucker by mistake?

I have to try! She hefted the heavy weapon and peered down the barrel. Her finger found the trigger.

Crack!

The rifle went off. The kickback knocked Andi backward. The cougar stood its ground. She'd missed! Tucker ran toward the cat again.

"Tucker, no!" Riley ordered, but the brave little dog did not obey.

Andi steadied herself for another shot.

Too late. The mountain lion swiped at Tucker than sprang. Riley screamed and fell under the cougar's weight.

Tears streamed down Andi's eyes. *Help me shoot straight, God,* she prayed. *For Riley's sake!*

Crack! Crack!

Andi let off two more rounds.

The cougar jerked and lay still. Andi dropped the rifle and collapsed to the ground. Her stomach heaved, and this time she could not stop her breakfast from coming up.

She wiped her face against her coat sleeve and sprang to her feet. "Riley!"

The cat lay sprawled on top of Riley. Tucker's teeth bit deeply into its hide. He shook his head back and forth and growled.

Andi made sure the cougar was dead before she fell beside it and began hauling the carcass away. It took all her strength to pull the cat off her husband. "Get away, Tucker," she demanded. "It's dead."

Tucker let go, yipped, and sat back on his haunches. He looked as proud as if he had killed the cougar all by himself.

Riley lay still, unconscious. His shirt was torn to ribbons. Several long, deep scratches raked his body from under his ear, along his neck, and across his chest. Another set of scratches— or were they bite marks—trailed down his torso. Blood flowed freely.

This much damage from one leap? It was horrifying.

Andi yanked Riley's shirt away. She knew if the cat had dug deeply enough, it could rip open a vein. Riley would die soon if that were the case.

Andi examined his wounds. Then she laid her ear next to his chest. His heart was beating slowly but regularly. *He's all right!* She sobbed quietly. *He's all right!*

Just then he groaned. "Riley!"

He opened his eyes. "Andi?" He groaned again and tried to sit up. "Did you get the cat?"

Andi nodded.

Cringing, Riley fell back to the ground. "It's bad, isn't it?"

"It could be better." Andi smiled through her tears. "You're scratched up pretty bad and losing a lot of blood."

She took a deep, shuddering breath. "But I don't think the cat did anything so bad that it can't be fixed with some bandages and rest."

Riley sighed. "Thank God. That was close. I thought I was a goner when the cat took that leap. Are you and Tucker all right?" He shifted his position to look at the dead cougar and yelped in pain.

"Lie still," Andi ordered. "Just stay put. I'm fine, and so is Tucker. I'm going to bring the wagon and get you back to the ranch."

Without waiting for Riley's answer, Andi leaped to her feet. Just as quickly, she sat down—hard. The world spun. Black spots swam before her eyes.

No wonder, she mused. *We forgot to eat the lunch I packed.*

Andi rose slower the second time. She told Tucker to stay with Riley and then carefully made her way to the wagon. Grabbing the horses' lines, she walked them back to where Riley lay unmoving.

The horses clearly smelled the cat. They twitched and shied and tossed their heads, but Andi kept them firmly under control.

"The cat's dead," she soft-talked to them. "Everything's all right. You can trust me." She stroked their noses and brought the wagon alongside the wounded Riley.

Between Andi's soft voice and the heap on the ground that didn't move, Ranger and Buster appeared to accept the fact that the predator they feared could not harm them, in spite of its terrifying scent. They finally calmed down and stood still.

Andi relaxed, but only for a minute. When she hauled the blankets out of the wagon and over to Riley, he looked worse than ever. His wounds needed attention, and soon.

Tucker hung over his master, whimpering and licking his face.

"Tucker, that's enough," Andi said. "Leave him be."

She poked around for Riley's knife and soon had one of the lighter-weight blankets hacked into strips. She wrapped his arms tightly and pushed another wool bandage against the bite mark on his shoulder.

Knowing Riley was not injured to the point of death did wonders for Andi's state of mind. Calmly and steadily, she bound up the rest of his wounds and prayed that no infection would set in before Doc Weaver could look him over.

Riley bore it with clenched teeth and a forced smile. "I love you," he whispered. "We'll get through this. The only sad thing is that I won't be able to finish cutting down that tree."

Andi laughed softly and planted a kiss on his cheek. "Don't worry about the tree. I'll get you home. And I love you too."

She rose. "I'll be right back with something to eat and drink. I don't know about you, but I'm so hungry I feel sick."

Riley nodded and closed his eyes.

A few minutes later, Andi hauled the two wicker baskets from the wagon and set them on the ground. She opened her mouth to say something cheerful to Riley, but the words froze in her throat.

Tucker was growling at a small animal nosing around Riley's unconscious body.

Chapter 5

Andi caught her breath. What was that thing? A badger? A bobcat?

The spotted animal let out a pitiful mew. Tucker yipped, clearly surprised, and sniffed it.

Andi's heart melted. A cougar cub!

No wonder the mountain lion had not run off, not even when gunshots had certainly scared it half to death. She was protecting her baby, and nothing would move her.

Tears sprang to Andi's eyes. *I killed its mother.*

It was too late to grieve over the loss of mama cougar. If she hadn't shot the cat, it would certainly have killed Riley.

But still, Andi had always loved kittens, and the poor creature mewing around its mother's dead carcass looked like a lost kitten—albeit a big one, perhaps six or seven weeks old.

Riley came first, however. Andi ignored the cub's pitiful cries and hurried to Riley's side. She unscrewed the top of her canteen and helped him drink draught after draught of the cool liquid. "You hungry?" she asked.

Riley made a face. "Not really. I just want to lie here and thank the good Lord I'm alive."

"Well, I'm starved." Andi dug around in the basket and drew out a sandwich, which she gobbled up in five quick bites.

Buried under the cloth-wrapped bundles, she found a battered coffee pot, a small jar of cream, and a packet of coffee. "Shall I kindle a fire and make you a hot cup of coffee before we start back? I even brought cream along, since I know how much you like it in your coffee."

No answer.

"Riley?" She turned and paused at the sight.

The cub had snuggled up next to Riley, who was petting it with his uninjured hand. His fingers scratched behind its ears. He didn't say a word. He could figure out as easily as Andi where this little fella had come from.

Tucker stood guard over them both.

"Poor little thing," Riley murmured.

"Poor little thing?" Andi put her hands on her hips. "His mother nearly killed you. I'm as sorry we stumbled into this as you are. I never meant to disturb a cougar and her cub. But what's done is done."

Andi winced. Since when had she become the voice of reason? As a child she was always bringing creatures home as potential pets. A blue-bellied lizard, a fuzzy tarantula, and once even a baby possum.

"Mama cougar was only trying to protect her young," Riley said softly. "Wouldn't you do the same, no matter if it cost you your life?"

Andi's heart skipped a beat. Yes, she would. She knew that now more than ever, but . . .

She shook her head to clear her thoughts and focused back on the present dilemma. "Coffee, Riley?"

Riley glanced up at the mid-afternoon sun. "No time to build a fire and brew the coffee, not if we want to make it back to the ranch before full dark." He took a deep, painful breath. "And you're going to have to push the horses to get us home at that."

Andi nodded her agreement and began to pile the foodstuffs back in the basket.

"Say, Andi," Riley said. "How about using some of that cream you meant for my coffee on this little fella?"

Andi sat back on her heels, jar of cream in her hand. Why not? She knew in her heart that the little cougar cub would be going home with them, at least temporarily.

It sure looked hungry. Riley's undamaged fingers were firmly tucked inside the cub's mouth. It sucked and sucked and sucked.

Andi unscrewed the lid and brought the container over. She dipped her fingers in the rich cream and coaxed the cub to transfer its loyalty from Riley to her.

It didn't take much coaxing. The moment the cub tasted the cream, it went crazy. It tried sucking the cream right from the jar. By the time the small creature's belly was full, it was purring and licking its whiskers. Thick white liquid covered its face.

Andi giggled. "We're stuck with it now."

"You know we can't leave him here in the middle of nowhere," Riley said, "with no mother to protect him."

He let out a deep breath. "I think I've rested long enough for the blood to stop oozing out of me. Let's go home."

It took all of Andi's strength to balance Riley. She knew good and well he was hurting much more than he admitted. When he stood, his face blanched. He staggered but caught himself before tumbling to the ground.

"I'm all right," he insisted between clenched teeth.

He wasn't, but it would accomplish nothing to make him admit it. Instead, Andi gritted her teeth and helped her half-crippled husband to the wagon. By the time he was settled onto the blankets in the wagon bed, he looked awful.

A moment later, he passed out.

Andi hurried back to the mewing cougar cub and snatched him up. Once he was settled next to Riley, the little feline curled up and fell asleep. His belly bulged.

Andi whistled. "Tucker, get in the wagon."

The dog obeyed and jumped in next to Riley. His eyes were alert. *You can depend on me,* he seemed to be saying.

Andi pulled herself wearily onto the wagon seat and picked up the reins. A dizzy spell threatened to overtake her, but she pushed it aside. Riley was depending on her.

"I can do this," she told the horses. "Let's go!"

The two horses leaped forward as one. Andi guided them around the young stands of trees, under branches of towering pines, and through narrow clearings in the forest.

Faster, faster, she urged them silently, but common sense kept her from letting the team move faster than a trot. Not over this rough ground.

But soon, very soon, she would push them for all they were worth.

Chapter 6

CIRCLE C RANCH, CALIFORNIA, DECEMBER 1886

By the time evening fell, Andi was out of the hills and headed for the Circle C ranch. The moment the trail widened out, she urged the horses faster, until they were badly lathered. Diego would have some harsh words for her treatment of *Señor* Riley's horses.

No matter. It couldn't be helped.

The horses would need a good rubdown after this abuse, but right now Andi had no energy left to worry about them. Only Riley mattered. A stab of uncertainty pierced her heart. Riley hadn't muttered a peep during the entire long, agonizing journey.

Andi kept the horses going at a fast gait. Thank God the rising moon was full. It lit the hills in stark, white light. *Home, home! Mother will take care of Riley. Chad will race to town for the doctor. And I can rest . . .*

Andi's arms felt like two lead weights. Her fingers grew numb from gripping the reins. The rest of her body was wracked with pain from jolting along. Not even the wide valley road felt smooth.

Poor Riley! He must be bouncing all over the place back there, even with the blanket padding.

Andi dared not stop to check on him. She knew the fastest route way to her childhood home, and she took it.

What felt like hours later, the lighted windows beckoned a cheerful welcome when she pulled into the long driveway. She slowed the horses down just long enough to cool them a smidgen then yanked them to a shuddering stop in front of the porch. Their sides heaved.

"Sorry, fellas," Andi apologized. She crawled down from the seat.

The instant her toes touched the ground, her legs collapsed. *Oof!* She sat down on the cold ground and huddled there, weary beyond belief. Every muscle ached.

In the distance, Andi saw cowhands mingling in the yard, but she was too tired to call out. It didn't matter. No one could miss the sounds of the jangling harnesses and pounding hooves tearing up the Circle C driveway. What's more, above all the racket, Tucker was frantically barking.

Someone would surely come.

A shout filled the air. Then a babble of Spanish and English voices grew closer. Sid McCoy led the group. When he saw Andi, he raised his lantern and lit into her like she was twelve years old again.

"What in tarnation's got into you, Miss Andi? Runnin' those horses like their tails are on fire? You shoulda—"

"Riley's hurt bad!"

Sid's eyes grew wide. He passed the lantern to one of the hands, ordered two others to help Miss Andi into the house, and leaped into the back of the wagon to see to his nephew.

"I'm fine," Andi insisted when Jake and Diego gently lifted her to her feet. She tried to brush them off.

Jake snorted. "Sure you are." He didn't let go.

"*No es la verdad, señorita,*" Diego muttered.

Andi gave in. Diego was right. It *wasn't* the truth. She felt far from fine. Nausea washed over her. She slumped and let the two cowhands carry her up the wide veranda steps.

Diego didn't bother to knock. He burst through the doorway yelling in Spanish.

The last thing Andi heard was Sid's astonished cry. "A cougar cub! What in tarnation . . ."

His voice faded, and Andi let sweet oblivion take her away.

***

"Riley!" Andi shot up from a terrifying nightmare. She had missed the shot. The cougar was mauling Riley. He was screaming . . . screaming . . . begging Andi to shoot the cat.

"Shh, sweetheart." Firm but gentle hands caught Andi before she could leap out of bed. "It's all right. Riley's fine. Chad fetched the doctor hours ago."

Andi threw her arms around Mother and took three long, deep breaths. "Really? Promise me he's all right."

Mother drew Andi's arms away and smiled. "I promise. Dr. Weaver said he's weak as a kitten from blood loss, but the cat did not tear into anything vital."

Tears of relief dripped down Andi's cheeks. "Thank you, God," she whispered.

"Yes, indeed," Mother agreed with a nod.

Andi threw aside the bedcovers. "I want to see him."

"It's the middle of the night." Mother replaced the covers. "He's sleeping peacefully"—she paused—"which is more than I can say about you." Her expression changed to one Andi knew well. A scolding was in the making.

Mother sat back in the overstuffed bedside chair. "I would like to know, daughter, what Riley was thinking today—letting you go off into the middle of nowhere. I always thought he was a sensible young man, but . . ."

She clucked her tongue, just like Aunt Rebecca used to do. *Uh-oh.* She winced. Mother sounded angry at Riley. *Very* angry.

Andi's eyes opened wide. "What do you mean, Mother?"

"Do not give me that innocent look, Andrea. You know exactly what I mean. I asked Dr. Weaver to look at you."

Andi didn't reply.

"I was worried," Mother went on. "You looked ghastly when Diego and Jake brought you inside. It's not like you to react like that—fainting and ill—from an all-day adventure in the mountains. Even if you did have to shoot a cougar."

"How did you know I shot the cat?"

"Oh, it wasn't hard for Chad to figure out. The used rifle, Riley's condition, an orphan cub." Her blue gaze bored into Andi. "Do not change the subject."

Andi swallowed. Did mothers know everything? Or did they just have ways of finding out what they wanted to know?

It would not have taken Dr. Weaver more than a minute to notice Andi's slightly bulging belly.

She ducked her head and fingered the blanket. "Riley doesn't know," she whispered without looking up. "I wanted to surprise him on Christmas Day about the baby."

"I see." Mother paused. "Well, that's the only good thing in all of this. My faith in Riley's good sense is restored."

She sighed. "What were you thinking, Andrea? You wanted a tree in the Circle C tradition. I understand that. But not at the expense of your little one."

"I felt *fine*," Andi protested. "And I'm—"

She broke off. She wanted to snap at Mother, to say she was a married woman now, and she could make her own decisions.

Andi knew better. She'd felt fine, but only until the trip turned upside down and demanded all her strength.

What if I'd ended up reacting like Lucy did when she was carrying Gracie? Lucy could hardly function at times. What if I couldn't take another step? What if I had keeled over while I was driving the wagon home? What if—

Mother caught Andi up in a tight embrace. "It's all right, sweetheart. All's well that ends well. But please, let this be a lesson to you."

Andi nodded.

Just then, Chad poked his head through the doorway. "Riley's awake. He wants to know if Andi's all right. I told him you were fine, but he's a stubborn one, that boy."

He grinned. "Better haul yourself out of bed for a few minutes, little sister, and assure my best wrangler that you're none the worse for your adventure."

This time Mother did not prevent Andi from flying out of bed. She drew on a housecoat and hurried to Riley's side in the guest room three doors down.

Riley's eyes lit up when he saw her. "You're all right."

"Yep." Andi smiled and sat down beside him.

Riley looked much better than he had earlier. The color was back in his face, and he was smiling.

Andi picked up his uninjured hand and squeezed it. Then she kissed his cheek. "I wanted to wait until Christmas, but I have something to tell you. I think it will help you heal faster."

She glanced toward the doorway. No one—not even Chad—was lurking about. She dared not wait for Christmas now. She didn't want her husband to be the last to know.

"Good news, I hope?"

Andi grinned. "Oh, yes." Nobody was spying, but she couldn't bring herself to shout her news out loud. She whispered in Riley's ear, "We're going to have a baby."

The tight squeeze on Andi's hand and his murmured "best Christmas gift ever" was music to Andi's ears. If he was angry that she hadn't told him before they left for their adventure, he was too much of a gentleman to bring it up.

Andi sat beside Riley and held his hand until his grip loosened. Then she slipped his hand under the covers, tucked the blanket around his neck, and brushed a kiss across his forehead. He was sound asleep, a contented smile on his face.

Andi suddenly felt more than fine. She tiptoed out of the room and made her way downstairs for a midnight cup of hot chocolate. To her surprise, Chad and Ellie were already there, sipping tea and chatting.

"I couldn't sleep," Ellie confessed.

"I'm glad you came downstairs, Andi," Chad said. "I need to talk to you. The men are in a quandary. They want to know what they're supposed to do with that cougar cub you hauled home."

Andi bit her lip. *Oh, dear! What am I supposed to do with it?*

Then a delightful idea tickled her thoughts. She knew the perfect recipient for the little Christmas cat.

She smiled at her brother. "I brought him home for you, Chad. Merry Christmas!"

NINE

OVERGROWN KITTY

MEMORY CREEK RANCH, CALIFORNIA, MARCH 1887

I've gotten myself into a real mess this time. What are we going to do with that cat?

Chapter 1

"That's it!" Chad Carter bellowed. "I've had it." His yell woke the baby, who wailed.

"For goodness sake, Chad," Ellie scolded her husband. "Can't you remember you're a father? Lower your voice."

Chad sheepishly tiptoed to the cradle and picked up his daughter. "I'm sorry about that," he whispered. "Shh."

He handed two-month-old baby Susie to Ellie then ran his fingers through his thick, black hair. "That cat has got to go. Today. I just found out the chickens are scattered from here to kingdom come."

His look turned grim. "That's not something I want to hear first thing in the morning, especially when I have a full day's work ahead of me."

"Kitty didn't kill any of the chickens, did he?" Ellie asked in a worried voice.

Chad shook his head and sat down on the edge of the bed. "But he might just as well have. They're so spooked they won't lay for a week. And do you remember what happened last week?"

He didn't give Ellie a chance to answer. "The ranch dogs chased the cougar into the cookhouse. He tried to get away from Duke and King and ended up on one of those high shelves. It snapped in two and—"

"I remember." Ellie broke into Chad's tirade, suppressing a giggle. "It was pretty funny."

Chad scowled. "It wasn't funny at all." He snorted. "A helpless, six-week-old cub is one thing. A thirty-pound cat is something entirely different. He thinks he's a person."

Kitty had grown incredibly fast the past three months. His spots were slowly beginning to fade. He followed Chad everywhere, spooking Sky, scattering the cattle, and startling the Circle C hands.

"Andi will be so disappointed," Ellie said. "Kitty was a Christmas gift."

Chad glowered at her. "I know. And like the complete fool I am, I kept the animal." He shook his head. "I should have said no right from the start. No matter how sorry I felt for Riley getting torn up by the cub's mother."

"I'm sure finding out your little sister is in the family way softened your heart too."

He gave Ellie a lopsided grin. "She did indeed catch me in a weak moment with that announcement."

His scowl returned. "It's been a long three months, my dear. This is a working ranch, not an animal menagerie. The cougar goes back to Andi and Riley today."

***

Andi was grooming Shasta when she heard the wagon pull up in the yard. She left her chocolate palomino tied to the hitching rail and hurried to see who her visitor might be.

Rounding the corner of the house, she stopped short. "Chad!"

She furrowed her brow. What was big brother doing here at the start of a workday?

The answer was not long in coming. At the sound of Andi's voice, Kitty's furry head popped up from the back of the wagon.

"Andi," Chad began. He sounded apologetic. "I hate to tell you this, but Kitty and the Circle C ranch are not made for each other. I can't keep him any longer."

Andi felt herself pale. "What do you mean? You're not going to . . . going to—"

"Perish the thought, little sister," Chad reassured her. "I wouldn't harm a hair on this cat's head."

Then what? Andi opened her mouth to ask, but Chad kept talking.

"This big cat has come to stay with you and Riley." He tugged on the makeshift leash, and Kitty sprang from the wagon bed.

Just as quickly, the cougar plopped onto the dirt at Chad's feet and stretched out. He looked perfectly content.

"Why?" Andi asked. "He looks harmless enough."

"Harmless, yes," Chad agreed. "I've never seen a more laid-back wild creature in my life." He winced. "But he's more trouble than I can keep track of, now that the spring ranch work is in full swing."

Andi sighed. She'd heard tales all winter about Kitty's antics, every Sunday during dinner. The stories kept the entire family in stitches.

"He's getting too big to keep corralled," Chad explained. "Mother doesn't want anything to do with him. Ellie is busy with the baby, and Mitch just throws up his hands when he sees the cat heading toward him for a belly rub."

He reached down and scratched Kitty's belly.

The cougar cub stretched out his legs even farther. Andi could hear the loud, rattling purr from where she stood.

Chad straightened up and held out the rope leash. "Here you go, little sister."

Andi reluctantly took the rope from her brother.

"Kitty's weaned," Chad said. "He doesn't eat that often. He prefers venison, although he'll eat mice and gophers in a pinch." His look turned grim. "I suggest you and Riley keep his diet free of beef or mutton."

Andi bit her lip. Yes, it would be best not to give the cougar a taste of easy beef. She nodded.

There didn't seem much to say. *Riley's going to have a fit,* she thought.

"Well, that's it then." Chad settled his hat more firmly on his head and climbed up on the wagon seat. "Good-bye, Kitty. Behave yourself."

The cougar ignored Chad. He rubbed his head against Andi's legs, clearly as content to be with her as he had been with Chad.

Swell.

Chapter 2

Andi was right. Riley did pitch a fit when he came home and found a cougar prowling around the yard. "Andi, what in the world—"

His yell was cut off by a frightened squeal. A thud and a groan propelled Andi out of the kitchen and down the back-porch steps.

"Oh, no!" Her hands flew to her cheeks in horror.

Dakota had thrown Riley and was bucking and kicking.

Kitty growled and took off running—straight for the barn. He disappeared inside. The sound of Shasta and the other horses in a panic poured through the wide-open doors.

When Andi peeked inside the barn, Kitty was perched in the hayloft. His front paws dangled over the edge of the loft. Straw and hay crowned his head. He saw Andi and yawned.

Safe at last, he seemed to be saying.

It took the livestock the better part of the evening to get used to the scent of a mountain lion roaming around.

Predator and prey. Never a good mix, no matter how docile Kitty acted . . . or no matter how much the cougar cub thought he was "one of the gang."

It took Riley even longer to come to an understanding with Kitty. "I should have seen this coming," he moaned while Andi dabbed away the blood on his forehead. He'd come down on a sharp rock.

"Ouch!" He jerked away.

"For heaven's sake, Riley," Andi snapped. "It's not like I asked Chad to bring Kitty here."

Riley sighed. "I know. I'm sorry."

Andi knew what her husband was thinking. They'd had no choice last December. Neither one of them was willing to leave the baby cougar to fend for itself in the wild. He was too young.

But now?

Kitty didn't know how to hunt. He had no mother to teach him. If Riley or Chad took him up to the Sierra, the cougar cub would perish.

It was as simple as that.

Riley reached up and squeezed Andi's hand. "We'll make do," he promised. "Let's just hope Kitty stays put until I can throw together a sturdy enclosure."

***

A week later, the cougar-tight enclosure was completed. It took both Andi and Riley pushing and shoving to convince Kitty to go inside.

The cougar did not like his new home at all. He paced. He scratched at the corner posts. He yowled mournfully.

Andi's heart melted. "He looks so sad cooped up."

"Would you rather Kitty was chasing the chickens or spooking the horses?" Riley shook his head. "It's a bad choice all the way around. But short of dumping him where we found him, I don't see any other solution."

Andi knew Riley spoke the truth. It still hurt, though.

As often as she dared, Andi released Kitty so he could romp in the yard. He liked best of all to sprawl out on the back porch next to Andi while she shelled peas or sewed baby clothes.

One rainy day, Andi brought Kitty inside. He took over the settee, which is where Riley found him that evening.

"Out he goes."

Yowling his protest, Kitty went back inside his enclosure.

The next morning, Riley and Andi stood in front of the enclosure. The *empty* enclosure. Riley yanked a broken plank from the top of the cage and sighed.

"Our curious cougar cub is on the loose."

Chapter 3

Kitty was gone two full days without a trace. "You have to find him," Andi pleaded with Riley. "He can't survive on his own."

She sniffed back her tears. "Worse, some farmer or rancher might shoot him. Kitty's friendly. He'll just walk right up to somebody. Then, *bang!*"

As it happened, there was no need for Riley to look for their overgrown, runaway kitten. Kitty showed up the third day. He was sitting at the back door one morning, when Riley went outside to saddle Dakota.

"Andi! Kitty's back!"

Andi rushed to the door. She knelt and threw her arms around the cub's furry neck. His rope collar was still in place.

Kitty licked Andi's face and started purring.

"You must be starved half to death," Andi murmured. "Stay right here."

She made her way inside to the icebox, where a small haunch of venison had been sitting for the past week. She brought it out and held it up to the cougar.

Kitty sniffed it and turned away. He was definitely not hungry.

The reason became clear a few minutes later.

Bang, bang, bang! It sounded like somebody was trying to break down the front door.

"Now what?" Riley wondered out loud. He left Andi and Kitty and hurried through the house.

Andi was only a few steps behind Riley. Kitty had squeezed through the screen door and was padding along at Andi's heels.

Riley swung the door open just as Vince Hollister's meaty fist came down for another blow. He stopped in mid-air.

"Good morning, Mr. Hollister," Riley greeted pleasantly.

"It ain't nothin' of the kind," Vince hollered. He peered past Andi and growled, "On account o' that . . . that *beast*." His eyes blazed.

Kitty yawned and scratched behind his ear.

"What do you mean?" Andi asked in a worried whisper.

Vince thrust a bloodied burlap sack under her nose.

143

"*This* is what I mean. Found what's left of one of m' newly born lambs early this morning."

Andi shuddered. Dizziness made her grab Riley's arm for support. The baby gave a protesting kick against the inside of her belly. She winced.

"Mr. Hollister," Riley began quietly, "what proof do you have that our pet cougar went after your sheep?" He wrinkled his brow. "For that matter, how do you even know about the cat?"

"Everybody in the valley knows y'all got yourselves a mountain lion," Vince growled. "Your range butts up against mine. It don't take too much figurin' t' know what done this."

Indeed, it did not, Andi agreed silently. She shot a glance at Kitty. He was washing his face, just like he'd finished a full meal.

This is terrible!

Vince dropped the gunny sack at Riley's feet. "If I so much as see a glimmer of that cat anywhere near my sheep, I'll shoot him on sight."

Vince turned on his heel and stomped off the porch. Then he mounted a dirty-gray horse and slammed his heels into his flank. "Y'all get rid o' that cat, ya hear?" he bellowed over his shoulder and galloped away.

Andi felt sick. The burlap sack mocked her. She turned away before her breakfast came up. "Do you think Kitty really took down a Hollister lamb?"

Riley shrugged. He guided Andi back inside and into the kitchen. "I'll take care of the remains in a minute. Let's sit down and talk."

Once at the kitchen table, Andi buried her head in her arms. "Kitty is too young to know how to hunt," she mumbled. "Couldn't a wolf have done it?"

"It's possible," Riley agreed. "But a newborn lamb isn't much of a hunt. Even a young cougar could carry it away."

"The neighbors didn't complain when Chad had the cat on the Circle C," Andi mourned.

"Our spread is much closer to the Hollisters," Riley said. "And the Circle C doesn't have any neighbors."

A loud purring noise brought Andi's head up. Kitty rubbed against her legs then settled under the table, where he began to wash himself in earnest.

Andi groaned. "Oh, Riley, what are we going to do?"

"It will take some serious thinking," he admitted. "The stronger Kitty grows, the less we'll be able to contain him. I thought I'd built that enclosure strong enough."

He sighed. "For now, keep Kitty with you. Don't let him wander off if you can help it. We'll lock him in a stall at night. That will keep him contained until we come up with a better solution."

Andi nodded. There was only one solution, but she didn't want to voice it out loud.

Kitty would have to be returned to the wild.

Chapter 4

Andi moped around the house for the next several days. She was so tired! It was hard to sleep at night. The noise from the barn rang with a cacophony of whinnies, yowling, and pounding.

The horses wanted out. Being so close to a predator kept them skittish and restless.

Kitty wanted out. Confined places made him scratch the stall posts nearly to smithereens. Loud thumps told Andi the cougar was leaping at the walls and door, trying to escape.

Poor Kitty!

Andi wished—not for the first time—that she hadn't talked Riley into that fateful Christmas tree adventure last December. If they'd stayed home, mama cougar and her baby would still be roaming the high country, as happy as two wild creatures had any right to be.

Andi had changed all that when she killed the mother. Now, it looked like the baby cougar would suffer the same fate.

Please, God, help us come up with a solution that saves Kitty's life, and at the same time keeps the livestock safe, Andi prayed while she washed the breakfast dishes.

She didn't expect an answer right away.

"Howdy!" A faint voice called from the front yard.

Andi wiped her hands on a towel and hurried to answer the door. When she stepped outside, a strange sight met her eyes. Sadie Hollister!

Andi hadn't seen her childhood friend in two years, not since she and Riley had ridden into the hills to talk to the Hollisters. She'd hoped their visit to the hillbilly family might shed some light on who was behind all the mischief that had broken out on the Circle C.

While not overly friendly, Sadie had shared what she knew about a stranger who asked too many questions. It had turned out to be Mateo Vega, one of the men who had brought grief to Andi and her family.

"Howdy yourself," she greeted Sadie. Why in the world had Sadie come to visit after so long?

A small, blond boy about the same age as Justin's boy sat on the saddle in front of Sadie. She yanked the dirty-gray horse to a standstill at the foot of the porch steps and dismounted.

Sadie helped the little boy off the horse and set him down on the ground. "Stay put, Jeffrey."

Jeffrey clung to Sadie's skirt and regarded Andi with wide, gray-blue eyes. He was dressed in a long, dirty nightshirt. His scraggly blond hair fell over his eyes.

He's a miniature version of Sadie, Andi thought.

"This-here's m' boy Jeffrey," Sadie volunteered. "I also got me a baby girl, Charlotte, but Ma's got her at home." She tossed her pale-blond hair from her face. "She's a screamer."

"I'm glad you dropped by," Andi managed.

"It's been a while since I seen ya," Sadie admitted.

Andi didn't know what to say. Sadie hadn't seemed too friendly that day two years ago, but she sure acted cheerful now. Why?

The girls had parted ways when they were about eleven years old. Andi never knew why. Sadie probably didn't know why either.

It just happened. It didn't help that Chad had never liked the Hollisters. He didn't like the idea of his youngest sister spending so much time with hillbilly riffraff. Eventually, Andi had gotten caught up in school, met new friends, and—

She shook her head. Childhood was over.

"It sure has been a long time," Andi agreed. "I'm married now, to Riley. You met him that time we rode up to your place a couple years ago."

"He seemed like a right-nice young fella."

Andi nodded. "We're expecting a baby either in late June or early July."

Secretly, she added, *Hopefully late June.* Andi wanted to have the baby in her arms when she headed to the Fourth of July festivities with Riley.

Sadie laughed. "I got eyes. It ain't hard to tell." Then she shrugged. "I reckon it happens to most gals sooner or later, but sometimes I wish I was still a kid . . ." Her words faded.

147

Andi didn't reply. She watched the little boy, Jeffrey, scuffle and fuss.

"Hush," Sadie barked. She sighed and turned her attention back on Andi. "You're probably wonderin' what I'm doing here."

The thought did cross my mind, Andi mused. Aloud she said, "What can I do for you? Would you like some tea? Coffee?"

Sadie shook her blond tangles. "Nah. I'm just rememberin' how nice you was to me all the time. Givin' me a cat, visitin' m' place. Fishin' with me, and even invitin' m' family to your rodeo an' all."

"I had fun too," Andi said softly. After all, Sadie had been a good friend all those years ago. Andi had needed a friend after Riley left the Circle C.

"Well . . ." Sadie drawled the words, as if she were too embarrassed to speak. Then she shrugged. "Thought I'd tell ya that Pa's mighty riled over that cougar cub y'all got here."

Andi nodded. "We heard from him already. I'm doing my best to keep Kitty close. I"—she swallowed—"I'm awfully sorry he got one of your lambs. We didn't think he was old enough to figure out how to go after prey. He hasn't any mother to teach him." She paused. "Are you sure it was Kitty?"

Sadie shrugged. She looked a lot older than Andi, like hard times had aged her more than it should. "I dunno. We saw a tawny blur and scared it off. Wasn't much left o' the lamb though."

She gave Andi a hard look. "Don't matter if it wasn't your cat. Pa's got it in his head that it's yours. He's gonna shoot it, Andi."

A soft yowl pulled Andi from Sadie's words. She opened the front screen door and let Kitty join them.

Sadie yelped and jumped back, yanking Jeffrey into her arms. "Get it away!"

Kitty plopped down at Andi's feet and purred.

Sadie's eyes nearly bugged out. Slowly, she relaxed.

"Kitty!" Jeffrey squealed. He wiggled down from his mother's arms and fell onto the cougar cub.

Sadie watched in obvious shock. "It's true," she whispered. "That mountain lion is as tame as a kitten. I never saw anythin' like it."

She reached out her hand and gave Kitty a tentative stroke.

When Sadie rose, Andi could tell her friend had fallen in love with Kitty. Her eyes were bright and sparkled. "I been thinkin', Andi. Remember that crazy fella, Loony Lou? The one who lived up in the mountains?"

"Yes."

Andi remembered Loony Lou, all right. She remembered him as if it were yesterday, even though ten years had passed. Sadie and her brother Zeke had turned back, scared to death to go into the woods where a crazy mountain man roamed. The Hollister kids had skedaddled home, leaving Andi and Cory to brave the dangers alone in their search for gold.

Loony Lou had been kind to her and Cory, letting them spend the night in his cabin when they'd lost their way. He'd tended Cory's injuries too.

But the mountain man was a strange one. He lived with his giant, furry black dog, along with a couple of bearskins he'd named Ebenezer and Methuselah.

Who named musty old bearskins, for goodness' sake?

"What about him?" Andi asked.

"I thought Loony Lou might be willin' to take care o' your cougar cub," Sadie said. "He could maybe keep him out of danger and—"

Andi gasped. What a grand idea! Loony Lou lived far enough in the wilderness to keep a lonely little cougar out of danger. Then a worried thought hit her. The mountain man was old when Andi and Cory stayed with him. He must be downright ancient by now.

She sighed. "What if he's not alive any longer?"

"It don't hurt none to find out."

"True," Andi agreed, frowning.

Riley would never let her travel so far into the wilderness to ask Loony Lou anything, not in her condition. She might be willing to go, but her adventure last December taught her that she'd better show a little more caution and good sense.

A small kick from the baby reinforced her decision.

When Andi didn't say anything more, Sadie took Jeffrey's hand. "I reckon I better get back. I just wanted to tell you that Pa's plum set on gettin' rid o' that cougar. I also wanted to give ya an idea 'bout what you could do."

Andi smiled. Sadie had shown her extraordinary kindness. She'd come all the way to Memory Creek to warn Andi about her father's intentions. "Thanks, Sadie. It's a wonderful idea."

Sadie gave Andi a bright smile. "Glad ya like it. Just came to me this mornin' when I was listenin' to Pa rant and rave 'bout the cougar. Knew I had t' warn ya."

"I'll tell Riley," Andi said. "Chad knows—or used to know—all about Loony Lou. If anybody can find him and talk him into taking Kitty, Chad can."

She bid Sadie and her little boy good-bye then settled herself on the porch steps. Kitty yowled and lumbered to her.

Goodness! Andi mused. His paws were certainly growing fast. They'd soon be the size of tea saucers.

The cat dropped down, rolled over, and spread all four legs. *Belly rub, please,* he seemed to be saying.

Andi giggled and obliged. She rubbed and rubbed. Then her eyes began to sting. *Oh, I am going to miss you, Kitty!*

Chapter 5

C had agreed that the Hollister girl's plan was sound. He and Riley left one bright Saturday morning. "There's no guarantee, but I haven't heard that the old man's dead," Chad told Andi. "He might still be kicking around up there. Like your friend Sadie said, it doesn't hurt to find out."

Andi held back tears and said her final good-byes to the cougar she and Riley had rescued last December. She buried her face in his fur and heard his rumbling purr.

"Come on, Kitty." Chad gave the rope leash a tug. The big cat obeyed, jumping into the wagon bed.

Andi kept watch until Riley, Chad, and Kitty disappeared around a hillock.

***

Late that afternoon, Chad and Riley returned to Memory Creek ranch. Andi strained her eyes to see if the wagon bed was empty, or if Kitty was being brought home.

"We found him," Riley announced when Chad pulled the wagon to a stop in front of the house. "Took most of the day, but it was worth it."

"Yep," Chad added. "The old man was eager to take the cougar off our hands—once we convinced him we weren't trespassers trying to move onto his mountain."

Riley chuckled. "That took some doing. We dodged a few shotgun cartridges before he stopped long enough to listen."

"He remembered you, Andi," Chad said.

"He did?" Andi grinned.

"Yep. He wanted to know how the 'tadpole' was doing. I told him you were going to have a tadpole of your own. Ol' Lou cackled when he heard that. Then he put down his gun and welcomed us like long-lost brothers."

"Best of all," Riley said, "he adopted Kitty. Looked to me like his eyes watered up when we told him about our plight. He actually swiped a sleeve across his face when he learned this was your idea."

Andi's heart swelled. Not only had she found a safe haven for Kitty, but she'd also made Lou happy.

"Yeah," Chad put in. "Come to find out, he'd lost Dog several weeks ago—just up and died of old age. He was grieving and told me it must've been the good Lord Himself that brought that cat to him."

They had not stayed long. After suggesting that Lou keep the cougar cub close by until the two of them had bonded, Riley and Chad left. They hiked along the creek until they found where they'd left the wagon.

"Then we came right home," Riley finished their tale.

"Are you sure Kitty and Lou will get along?" Andi asked. She already missed the cub dreadfully.

Chad laughed. "Oh yes, little sister. When we left, Kitty was sprawled over Lou's lap, purring to beat the band. Lou was scratching the cat's belly and promising him a haunch of deer for supper."

Tears welled up in Andi's eyes. *Thank you, Lord. You answered my prayer in a way I never imagined.*

Andi would probably never see the cougar cub again, but Kitty was safe. By the time Lou grew too old to care for him, the cougar would have certainly adjusted to the wild and become the king cat he was created to be.

LAMB TROUBLE

MEMORY CREEK RANCH, CALIFORNIA, MAY 1887

I've wanted a lamb ever since I was a little girl.

Chapter 1

Andi shook out the rug and shaded her eyes. A swayback, dirty-gray horse was trotting patiently up the lane.

She didn't recognize the horse right off. Memory Creek ranch was off the beaten path, and the only visitors Andi and Riley usually saw were family and friends.

"Hey, Andi!"

Andi's heart leaped to her throat. Sadie Hollister. What was she doing here?

Andi couldn't help being grateful for the way Sadie had helped solve the cougar cub problem two months ago. Her suggestion of giving the cub to Loony Lou was brilliant, and a true blessing.

According to Riley, the old hermit's eyes had lit up when he learned the little mountain lion needed a home. He'd been lonely since the passing of his canine companion, Dog. Kitty and Loony Lou had taken to each other like bread and butter.

Andi lifted a friendly hand. "Hey yourself, Sadie."

During her last visit, a small, blond boy had perched in front of Sadie. Today she rode alone.

Sadie brought the horse to a standstill at the foot of the porch steps. She dismounted and untied a burlap sack that was looped around her saddle horn.

"How have you been?" Andi asked. She warily eyed the sack. Sadie's father had delivered an unpleasant surprise in a burlap sack just like this one. What was Sadie up to?

"Fair to middling," Sadie chirped. "And yourself?"

Andi laid a hand over her belly. "Mostly tired all the time. What brings you to Memory Creek this morning?"

Sadie grinned. "I remembered it's your birthday."

Really? Sadie had never remembered Andi's birthday before. Well, once maybe. Andi had turned ten that May, when she returned home from her stay in the city with Aunt Rebecca. Sadie insisted on having a tea party under the oak tree by the creek to celebrate Andi's birthday.

The oak tree was still there, right in Andi's backyard.

"Why, thank you." She wracked her memory to think of Sadie's birthday. No luck.

"I figured it was a good excuse to come callin'." She shrugged. "I ain't been very neighborly. Got too much on my mind with my fractious young'uns."

Sadie looked around. "It's real nice you got your own place here, right next to the creek where we used to fish." She held out the sack. "Never mind. I brung ya somethin'."

Just then a tiny *baa, baa* sounded through the rough weave of the sack.

Andi caught her breath. "A lamb!" Her heart thrummed. She tore away the string and withdrew the small creature. It looked to be no more than a week old.

"I love lambs," Andi said, cuddling it.

"Don't I know it," Sadie agreed. "But your brother never let you keep any."

The years fell away. Andi had just won a little black lamb at the State Fair in Sacramento.

"Where did this animal come from?" Chad asked.

"I won him," Andi explained. "His name is Inky. He drinks from a bottle."

"You can't keep him."

"I can too! I won him with my fair ticket. I'm taking him home."

Chad crossed his arms. "No, you're not."

In the end, through tears, Andi had taken the lamb back. It had been her own decision, but it still hurt.

A few years later it had happened again.

"So, this lamb belongs to you," Chad said. He held Snowball at arm's length. "Where in the world did you get it?"

"From Sadie. She traded me for the cat I gave her."

"Ohhh. Andi, I hate to tell you this, but the lamb has to go back to the Hollisters."

And it did.

Andi smothered a defiant smirk. Ha! Chad was nowhere around. Best of all, he was not Andi's boss any longer. Chad could only boss the Circle C, not Memory Creek ranch. He had no say-so about what she could keep as a pet and what she couldn't.

No sirree!

"Thank you, Sadie." Andi stroked the prickly wool. The lamb bleated and nudged her hand with its nose.

"Can you keep him this time?" Sadie scowled. "Or is that bossy brother of yours still tellin' ya what to do?" She sighed. "If you can't keep him, well, Pa's gonna butcher him. He and Ma don't like runts."

"Oh, *no*, Sadie! We can't let that happen. Riley's a lot different than Chad. He'll let me keep him."

"So, your man is all right with having this lamb hanging around the yard?"

Andi nodded and cuddled the lamb.

Sheep and cattle don't mix. A little voice whispered the words Andi had heard so often growing up. *And I still live on a cattle ranch.*

Her fingers closed around the small, underfed animal. But here was the lamb she'd always wanted, and no one could make her get rid of him. Not even Riley.

Deep down, Andi's conscience pricked her. A wife should try to be reasonable. She should submit to her husband's wishes, especially if he felt strongly about it. *I'll ask Riley later. We always talk things through. I'll convince him.*

Riley had never liked sheep, not even when he was a boy living on the Circle C. He'd turned his nose up at the lamb she'd won at the fair. *"Lambs are cute, but they grow up to be stinky sheep."* Such truth from an eight-year-old boy.

It doesn't hurt to ask. I know he'll agree. Andi soothed her conscience and considered the matter settled.

Sadie didn't stay long. "Can't leave those two ornery young'uns with Ma for long." She mounted the gray horse and rode off. "Happy birthday!" she called over her shoulder.

Andi named the lamb Jasper and carried him to an empty stall in the barn. She coaxed a cup of milk from their cow, filled a glass bottle she scrounged from the tack room, and fed the lamb. With his belly full, Jasper flopped to the straw and fell asleep.

Andi took her own nap. She awakened to Riley gently shaking her shoulder. "Hey, sleepyhead."

Andi shot up. "Oh, dear. How late is it?"

Riley didn't reply. Instead, he pulled her off the settee and suggested she change into a fresh dress.

Half-asleep, Andi stumbled to do as he asked. "Why? Where are we going?"

"Never mind that, birthday girl." Riley's eyes twinkled. "Just dress and get in the buggy."

"Don't you want supper?" Andi gave him a cocky grin. "I can whip up some bread and butter."

"Nope. I've got something better in mind."

Something better than Andi's cooking? Well, that didn't take much. She smothered a chuckle and hurried out to the buggy.

Chapter 2

Happy birthday!" The shouts erupted the instant Andi and Riley stepped through the door of the Circle C ranch house.

Andi gasped. The whole family stood in the foyer. Mother, Justin and his family, Chad, Ellie, and baby Susie. Melinda and Peter. Mitch had even brought Emily McConnell to the celebration.

The only missing family members were her sister Kate and the kids. Of course, now that Troy had turned himself in, the Swanson family was probably too busy visiting San Quentin to take time off for a birthday party in the valley.

That was fine with Andi. She was more than happy that Troy was on his way to putting his life back together. Two more years, and he would be out of prison, hopefully for good.

Mother swallowed her daughter in an embrace, and everyone began talking at once. Three-and-a-half-year-old Sammy squealed and jumped up and down. "Happy birfday, Andi! Happy birfday!"

The chaos was eventually brought under control, and the family sat down to eat supper.

Nila and Luisa had outdone themselves fixing Andi's favorite foods. Fried chicken, mashed potatoes and gravy, biscuits and jam. A big pitcher of lemonade joined the banquet.

Supper was delicious, especially compared to some of the meals Andi had prepared lately. Usually by the end of the day, she was too tired to put much effort into making a meal. She rubbed her ever-expanding belly and hoped Baby Prescott made an appearance right on time.

Andi ate and ate. Riley also seemed to be making up for the famine at Memory Creek ranch. He refilled his plate more than once.

Andi's heart overflowed with gratitude. This get-together was better than any birthday gifts. Speaking of gifts . . .

"Sadie Hollister dropped by today," Andi began. "She brought me a birthday gift."

Chad raised an eyebrow. "Oh?"

Andi knew by the look in his eye that he might suspect where this was going.

"She brought me a lamb," Andi finished with a grin. "The cutest one ever."

Dead silence.

Chad looked at Riley. "Did you know about this?"

Riley stared at Andi. He shook his head.

Mother opened her mouth to speak then closed it.

"You can't keep a sheep here, Andi." Chad sounded firm.

"Of course not here. At Memory Creek. I don't live on the Circle C anymore," Andi reminded her brother.

Chad didn't answer, which was a pleasant surprise. Andi had him there.

She let out a breath and looked around the table.

"Here's the pet I've always wanted. Isn't *anyone* in favor of my keeping him?" She glanced at her husband. "Riley?"

Another round of silence.

Indecision covered Riley's face.

"You too, Riley?" Andi sighed.

"I'm not your boss, either, Andi," he said quietly. "I'm your husband. But I'm asking you with all gentleness to get rid of the lamb. You know—"

"That sheep and cattle don't mix," Andi finished. "I know. But, Riley, it's only one little lamb. I've wanted a lamb all my life. Please may I keep him?"

Riley looked at Chad, who shook his head.

"No," Riley said. "I prefer you didn't."

Andi winced. Riley's words stung.

An ominous silence settled over Andi's birthday supper. No one spoke. No one moved.

Then Mother suggested that they should cut the cake. "It's your favorite, Andrea—chocolate."

Without waiting for a *yea* or *nay* from her daughter, Mother hurried into the kitchen. She returned with a double-layered chocolate cake with nineteen lit candles. The family sang "happy birthday" with all their hearts, but Andi could feel the strain.

Somehow, her perfect birthday party had dissolved into a possible family feud.

All on account of one little lamb.

Chapter 3

Riley and Andi returned home in silence. A part of Andi's mind knew Riley was right. Most cattle ranchers didn't run sheep. For sure the Circle C ranch didn't, and Memory Creek ranch ran alongside the Circle C.

Goodness! Memory Creek used to *be* the Circle C.

Another part of Andi's mind screamed that she was right too. One little lamb would not ruin the vast rangeland. Even a thousand sheep couldn't make a dent in the grazing land.

So, why is Riley being so stubborn? Andi sulked. Mother had pointed out many times before that *"sulking is unseemly,"* but Andi was mired in self-pity. *Jasper is my pet. The lamb I've always wanted. And no one is going to take him away from me.*

A twinge of guilt pinched her thoughts. This was not the right attitude. Not by a long shot. But she shoved her good sense into a corner and refused to budge.

Riley tried his best to be patient and reasonable. He and Andi sat up past midnight talking it over. He explained all the reasons that keeping Jasper was not a good idea.

Andi had heard the reasons before, so his words sounded like the drone of bees in her head.

Riley fell silent.

Andi took the opportunity to unleash her fury. "What's so wrong with keeping *one little lamb?*"

Riley let out a breath. "Didn't you hear anything I said?"

Truth be told, no, she hadn't. His words were a buzz. Besides, Andi had been too busy steaming.

Be angry and sin not, her conscience whispered.

She ignored those well-worn and familiar words. "I've always wanted a lamb. Chad was too mean and bossy to let me keep one."

She dug her fingernails into her palms and fought to keep her voice under control. "It's not fair!"

Andi cringed. That was the cry of a spoiled child. She'd used those three words too many times growing up. They'd never gotten her anywhere back then. She wasn't sure they'd get her anywhere tonight either.

Silence.

"I'm going to bed," Andi said at last, her voice stiff and low. "Thank you for the party."

She couldn't bear to sit here one minute longer under Riley's frustrated and sorrowful gaze. *No sirree!* She was right this time.

Andi stalked from the sitting room and headed to the bedroom. Her eyes burned hot, and her throat was tight from holding back tears. She undressed and readied herself for bed.

You're acting foolishly, her heart told her. *Riley is only doing what's best.*

But I love Jasper, Andi argued back. *And I don't want to see the poor creature butchered.*

You love Riley more.

Riley came to bed. "G'night, Andi."

Andi ignored him and rolled over. He didn't understand. Worse, she was sick and tired of being in the family way. This lamb was a perfect distraction to take up the last weeks of waiting for the baby to arrive. Couldn't Riley see that?

Tears trickled down her cheeks. It was the first time since they'd been married that Andi didn't say good-night to Riley. She burrowed under the covers and silently cried herself to sleep.

***

The next two days felt like two years. Andi took care of Jasper, but the joy of having a lamb began to wear off.

Riley tried to talk with her, but each time she cut him off. "You don't understand. You'll *never* understand. You're as mean as my brother."

Those stinging, horrid words just sprang from Andi's lips. Worse, they were not true. Riley was kind and gentle, and he never bossed her.

The baby went into conniption fits whenever Andi yelled. He rolled and kicked as if to say, "Don't yell at my daddy."

Andi and Riley ended up avoiding each other. It hurt, more than Andi ever thought it would. But her own sinful stubbornness hurt even worse.

What was the matter with her? *You're having a baby*, a comforting voice soothed. Maybe that was a reason, but it certainly was not an excuse.

Andi began to wish she'd never seen Sadie and that lamb.

That evening, Andi rose from the rocking chair and went to bed early. Riley could stay up all night as far as she was concerned. But she couldn't sleep.

She turned up the lamp and grabbed the closest book. Andi expected to see *Five Weeks in a Balloon* in her hand, but it wasn't.

It was the Bible.

Fingers shaking, Andi opened to the bookmark—where she'd left off maybe a week or two ago. The heading above James three made her flush. *Taming the Tongue*.

Never in Andi's life did she want to slam a book closed so fast, but she didn't. Instead, her gaze was pulled to the verses. "And the tongue is a fire, a world of unrighteousness . . . It is a restless evil, full of deadly poison."

Andi's heart squeezed. The verses shouted their message. She cringed when she remembered her heated words over the past few days.

Not to mention the "why don't you just sleep in the barn" arrow of deadly poison she'd hollered at Riley this evening.

All because of a silly childhood desire to keep a lamb.

What a wretch I am! Andi had disobeyed God. She'd gone on a rant worse than any she'd experienced from her older brother through the years. She hadn't sought the Lord's counsel on whether having a lamb was a good idea. After all, her time would soon be taken up with caring for a baby.

Andi bowed her head. Nobody had to tan her hide for her selfishness. Her conscience was doing a terrific job of waking her up to her shortcomings.

I wasn't willing to even listen to Riley. I thought only of myself. She set the Bible down and sent up a short but heartfelt apology. If only she could learn this lesson once and for all!

Then Andi prayed for courage, because as much as she wanted to make things right with Riley, stubborn pride kept trying to rear its ugly head.

I will do this, Andi determined. She climbed out of bed, pulled on her housecoat, and left the bedroom.

Riley wasn't in the sitting room. He wasn't looking around for a snack in the kitchen. Where was he? It was getting late.

Andi slid on her boots and made her way to the barn.

She found Riley in the tack room, working on a bridle. He was fiddling with it but seemed distracted. More than once he laid the piece of tack down, sighed, and bowed his head.

He didn't sense Andi's presence.

She looked around the tack room. A narrow cot had been set up in a corner. A saddle blanket lay across it. *What in the world? Surely, Riley doesn't think I really meant it—*

Her stomach turned over, and it wasn't Baby Prescott rolling around. Riley was really and truly going to sleep in the barn? Under a dusty saddle blanket? *No!*

SUSAN K. MARLOW

Andi clasped her hands together and cleared her throat.

Riley turned his head. His eyes widened. "I thought you went to bed."

A sob caught in her throat. "Oh, Riley!"

Riley dropped the bridle and hurried over. He wrapped Andi in a tight hug and led her over to the cot. "Sit down."

Seeing the cot in the corner, and Riley all alone, tore down the wall of pride in Andi's heart. She'd been wretched to her sweet husband, and he'd taken it like a true gentleman.

"I'm sorry," Andi said. "I've been horrible to you."

Riley held her close. He didn't say anything.

"I put a sheep before my husband." She hiccupped and swallowed hard. "A *sheep*, for goodness' sake."

Riley's lips curved upward. "And a scrawny one at that."

Andi choked, trying hard not to laugh. Leave it to Riley to make her laugh, even in the worst of times. "I was reading in James, and I came to my senses."

She fingered the saddle blanket lying on the cot. It was stiff and smelled like sweaty horses. *Ugh.* "I don't really want you to sleep out here."

"I know." Riley smiled. "I forgive you. How could I not? I love you."

Andi buried her face in his shoulder. Her tears flowed, hot and stinging. But this time they were tears of release. "I love you too."

When she sat up and sniffed, Riley handed her a bandana. "You never have one when you need it." He chuckled, and Andi knew everything was all right in her world again.

Riley helped her up. "It's getting chilly. Let's go inside."

With one last glance back at the forlorn cot, Andi walked back to the house. Once inside, she brewed some tea and they sat at the kitchen table.

Andi wasn't tired any longer. She felt energized and wide awake. Riley, on the other hand, looked brooding, and much too quiet.

"What are you thinking about?" she asked.

"Your lamb."

Andi nodded. "I'll ask a ranch hand to take the lamb back to Sadie in the morning. Maybe she can hide it or something to avoid the butcher block."

Riley shook his head. "No, Andi. It's not that. I guess I never realized how much a lamb would mean to you." He sighed. "I thought it was something from your childhood, something you couldn't let go of—like an ongoing battle between you and Chad."

"You're partly right," Andi said, "but I did always love little lambs."

"I've let Chad influence me too much in this," Riley admitted. "I have nothing against sheep."

Andi raised her eyebrows. "Really? You called them stinky when you were a little boy."

"Uncle Sid's doing, I'm sure," Riley scoffed, chuckling.

He turned serious. "I've done a lot of thinking over the past few days. I think Chad and Sid have pounded this whole sheep and cattle issue into the ground, and I went along with it. I dug my stubborn heels in, based on somebody else's convictions, which aren't necessarily my own."

Andi's heart raced. What was Riley getting at?

He took a deep breath. "I'm not going to let Chad—or any other cattleman—determine what I do on Memory Creek ranch. I don't believe one little lamb will destroy this ranch."

"You mean . . ."

Riley nodded. "You may keep the lamb for now, but—"

"Oh, Riley, thank you!" Andi squealed.

"*But*," Riley repeated, "if anything goes wrong, anything *at all*, you're giving this whole thing up. I don't want to give Chad any excuse to tease either one of us on account of one silly, bleating sheep. Agreed?"

Andi nodded. "Nothing will go wrong. You'll see."

"We will also return to this subject once the baby arrives. A lamb and a baby may be too much for a new mother."

"Sure. That's fine." Andi was too happy to think that far ahead. *Oh, Jasper, what fun we'll have!*

Chapter 4

Andi kept Jasper in the barn, but he soon became cramped and unhappy. He bleated all day long. He wanted out. His bleats and hoofbeats could be heard every time Andi stepped outside.

Finally, in desperation, she released him from his prison and let him romp around the yard. He nibbled at the grass, but mostly he followed Andi around.

"Andi had a little lamb . . ." she chanted. So sweet.

Jasper was sweet, but the rest of Andi's days of late were anything but sweet. She laid a hand over her belly and sighed. *I'm hot. I'm fat. I'm tired.*

She wished all this "in the family way" business was over.

"I want my mother," Andi whispered more than once over the next few days. "I want to be Andi Carter again and hop on Shasta. I want to gallop to my special spot and—"

She broke off. Oh, wait. She was already living at her special spot, but it didn't feel as special as it used to. Not with a basket full of newly sewn baby items that needed washing.

The grownup thing to do would be to wash and hang the clothes. Sighing, Andi set herself to the task.

An hour later, baby clothes, diapers, and blankets were pinned up, flapping in the breeze. The rest lay in the wicker basket, ready to join the other items on the clothesline.

The sudden *clop, clop, clop* of a horse and buggy pulled Andi from her task. A visitor!

She dropped what she was doing and hurried around the house. "Hi, Ellie," she greeted her sister-in-law. "I'm so glad you came by."

Baa, baa! Jasper leaped and bounded between them.

Andi ignored the lamb. She led Ellie and baby Susie up the steps and into the house, shutting the door on Jasper.

Riley might tolerate a lamb on Memory Creek ranch, but he would not be so forgiving if he found him inside the house.

Ellie laughed. "I see you still have that lamb. Chad told me all about it."

"I bet he did." Andi scowled. It was none of big brother's business.

Jasper clip-clopped around the porch and bleated. Eventually he gave up, and peace was restored.

Ellie stayed for an hour. Her visit was like a fresh, cool breeze. When she left, Andi placed the tea things in the dishpan and glanced out the back window. Then she gasped. The baby clothes!

Andi slammed through the screen door, clomped down the steps, and hurried to the clothesline. "Oh, no!"

Not one bib or gown was left inside the basket. Not one diaper. The other baby items swung in the breeze, thankfully, but the rest of the clothes, blankets, and diapers were scattered across the dry, dusty yard.

Andi didn't have to look far to find the culprit. "*Jasper!*"

He ran around the corner. A white something hung from his mouth. A tiny bonnet.

"No!" Andi snatched the bonnet away and cringed. It was chewed up, and so full of dirt it might never come clean.

Jasper looked at her with black marble eyes and bleated as if to say, *What did I do?*

"Bad lamb. Bad, bad, bad." Andi choked on a throat full of tears and scooped him up. "Back in the stall you go."

She dumped Jasper in the barn and wearily returned to collect the ruined items. Some were so torn and filthy they had to be thrown away.

"I hate to sew!" Andi wailed. She had so little time to sew replacements. The baby was due in less than a month.

Tired and furious, she pumped fresh water and rewashed the clothes she could salvage. Afterward, she pinned them up good and tight. Overcome with weariness, she dragged the empty laundry basket up onto the back porch.

"I'm done with that!" Andi couldn't look at another piece of soiled laundry. She gave the basket a toss. It flipped over and landed upside down under the kitchen window. Andi let it lie and stumbled indoors.

She couldn't help but shed a few hot tears at the thought of all her hard work. Gone. All because of one little lamb. She blinked and swiped away her tears. It wouldn't do to let Riley see her in this state.

Not if she wanted to keep Jasper.

Chapter 5

The next day, Andi felt refreshed. She forgave Jasper of his mischief and let him out for a romp. After all, the poor little fella didn't know he'd done wrong.

Andi sat on the porch and watched the lamb leap and run. She laughed at his antics. She rubbed his tight wool curls and scratched between his ears. "You're so cute!"

Yesterday, Ellie had left Andi with enough dried apples to make a pie. Why not? The June morning was not as hot as usual, and Riley would love an apple pie for supper.

Andi soaked the apples and then rolled out the pie dough. She smiled. A flaky pie crust was one of her few baking accomplishments. She hummed a little tune as she worked.

The golden, bubbling apple pie came out of the oven looking twice as delicious as it had before baking. Andi's mouth watered at the rich, apple-cinnamon scent.

"Won't Riley be pleased!" The pie was perfect in every way. A crisp crust, gooey center, and golden top. "It will make a great supper."

She grinned. Like two errant children, she and Riley would devour the whole pie.

Andi opened the kitchen window and set the pie on the sill to cool. The summer breeze wafted over the pie and spread its sweet smell into the entire house.

Wait until Riley walked in and smelled this treat!

***

A *clang* and a *splat* woke Andi from a light doze. She bolted upright from the settee, tossing *Five Weeks in a Balloon* to the floor. What was that noise?

She ran into the kitchen. Her gaze flew to the windowsill. The *empty* windowsill.

"Where's my pie?" Andi leaned over the counter and looked out the window. "Oh, no, no, no!"

Her beautiful, state-fair-perfect pie lay in a gooey heap all over the porch. Worse, the yellow jackets had found it. A dozen of the pesky hornets buzzed above and around it. A few more were walking all over it, sucking up what was supposed to be her supper.

Baa, baa!

Andi was so focused on the bees that she didn't see Jasper at first. She leaned as far over the counter as her belly would let her and stuck her head farther out the window.

The lamb stood a few yards away. Sticky pie filling and golden crust splattered his face and front legs.

"Jasper!" Andi pushed away from the counter and banged through the screen door. "Look what you've done, you naughty creature!"

First the clothes. Now the pie. But how in the world had Jasper reached the pie? Then she saw it. The wicker laundry basket lay on its side halfway across the porch. "You are not a goat!"

No, he wasn't. A goat would have made clean work of the pie. A goat would have stood on the overturned basket and eaten the pie right off the sill. A goat would not have spilled a crumb.

But not Jasper. He was too clumsy—too much of a sheep— to keep his balance.

For a moment, Andi understood Chad's frustration. Then she quickly shoved her irritation away. It wasn't Jasper's fault he was a curious little lamb.

Andi took him back to the barn. Maybe Riley could rebuild the paddock he'd made for Kitty—an escape-proof enclosure this time.

Jasper could have fresh air but not get into the baby clothes or a pie.

She winced. Riley had taken the other paddock apart not long after Kitty found a new home in the wilderness. Would he want to start all over again? Well, it wouldn't hurt to ask.

Andi cleaned up the lamb and took him to his stall. Then she headed back to the porch to clean up the pie. She stopped short. Worse and worse! The yellow jackets had found all their friends and relatives and were feasting on the sweet, sticky mess.

Andi let them feast. She had no interest in getting stung over a pie.

When Riley returned from repairing fences, he had questions. He wanted to know why there was no supper. He also wanted to know why a swarm of bees was buzzing around a wet spot on the back porch.

Andi was too tired to answer. When most of the bees had their fill, she'd brought in the pie pan and washed it up. She threw a bucket of water on the bees and what was left of the pie crumbs.

Riley ate bread and milk that night, and Andi went to bed.

Chapter 6

I s something wrong?" Riley asked the next morning.

Andi smeared jam on her toast. "Why do you ask?"

"Let's see . . ." Riley stirred sugar into his coffee and eyed her. "You're looking more tired than I've ever seen you. Last night you went right to bed without supper. You've also been acting more—" He cleared his throat and looked away.

"Grumpy?" Andi sighed. "I reckon I have been."

"Why?"

"For one, there's this baby." She patted her belly. "He or she won't let me sleep at night and wears me out during the day. Then"—she swallowed—"there's Jasper."

"More mischief?"

Andi nodded. "He ruined some of the new baby clothes."

Riley winced. He clearly knew sewing was not Andi's favorite task. "Ouch. That must have hurt. I'm sorry."

"Not as sorry as I am," Andi said. "I can't keep track of him. Yesterday, he knocked our supper off the windowsill."

"Ohh . . ." Riley smiled. "Is that why I had milk and bread for supper? I figured you'd burned the food or—"

"Oh, Riley, *don't*." Andi buried her face in her hands. Riley's harmless bantering usually made her laugh. Not today.

Riley immediately turned concerned. "I'm sorry, Andi. I was only teasing."

"I know, but right now—"

"Boss!"

Andi and Riley leaped up and ran for the back door.

A ranch hand ran around the yard hollering. "Call off this stinkin' sheep, boss! He won't stop chasing me."

Bleating loudly, Jasper bounded after Ross. The other two hands stood nearby, laughing their heads off.

Riley slammed the screen door open and took the porch steps in one leap. "Jasper! Come here, boy."

The lamb ignored him. Instead, Tucker flew from the barn, tail wagging.

Andi laughed. "Jasper is not Tucker. Let me find some bread and honey. He loves that treat."

There was no need for the treat. When Andi returned, her fingers holding a piece of bread, Riley was scratching Jasper's head and talking to him.

"How on earth did you—"

"Animals like me," Riley quipped. "I went after him, and he came right to me." He looked at Ross. "What happened?"

"I'm sorry, boss. I let him out. He acted so friendly that I let him nibble my breakfast." He held out a piece of toast lathered in honey. "I reckon he wanted more."

Andi's cheeks heated. She'd trained Jasper to like bread and honey. She often held a treat in her hand and taught him to follow her. Jasper had learned his lesson too well.

The lamb bleated and tried to get away, but Riley hung on. "It might be best to leave Jasper in his stall."

"Yes, sir." Ross walked off, mumbling under his breath.

Andi winced. Their cowhand sounded just like Chad.

She knelt beside Riley. "Tell me the truth. How did you get Jasper to come to you so quickly?"

"I told you. Animals like me."

"C'mon, Riley. There's more to it than that. Tell me."

"All right." He looked sheepish. "If you must know, I've been spending time with Jasper. He's a cute little rascal, if a bit smelly and troublesome."

He chuckled. "I've watched you leading him around the yard, and I began to do the same. A bit of sweet grain goes a long way." He scratched Jasper's head. "I like him."

Andi's laughter bubbled up. "Don't tell Chad."

"Never." He winked. Then he let Jasper go, and the two of them romped around the yard.

Chapter 7

The promise Andi made to Riley blared loudly in her head over the next few days. *"If anything goes wrong, anything at all, you're giving this whole thing up."* Truth be told, she wanted nothing more than to follow through with that promise.

Jasper had turned out to be more trouble than he was worth. Before Andi knew it, she was sick and tired of sheep. She was so sick of them that she was ready to apologize to Chad for all the times she'd hollered at him for not letting her keep the bothersome creatures.

Andi should have listened to her big brother and to her husband that first night. *I can't believe I wanted to keep Jasper.*

Now she was stuck with a lamb that looked and acted more like a sheep than a cute lamb. But she didn't dare admit to Riley she wanted the lamb to go.

Riley had become more attached to Jasper than Andi ever would have thought possible. They were like two peas in a pod. Jasper followed Riley everywhere, right there alongside Tucker. He fed Jasper sweet grain until the lamb's belly nearly scraped the ground.

How could she tell Riley that Jasper had to go?

Riley didn't miss much. He clearly knew something was up, but Andi always answered his questions with, "It's the baby."

Yeah, she added silently, *the baby lamb.*

Two days later, Jasper went missing.

It was late afternoon. By this time, Jasper was usually by the barn, ready to curl up for a nap in the stall or eat a little treat if he'd been good that day. But he wasn't there.

Andi let out a long, frustrated breath. Tired and hungry, she didn't want to chase down a lamb.

He could be anywhere, she thought wearily.

She sighed and began the search. She wandered behind trees, around the barn, and near the creek. No matter how hard she called, Jasper didn't appear. He didn't bleat.

Worry crept into Andi's thoughts. Even with Jasper's mischievous ways, he never wandered far. "Jasper!"

It was getting late. Maybe Riley could give her a hand with the search after supper. She turned back and headed for the house.

Then she stopped. Mixed in with Jasper's small tracks on the ground were other tracks. She knelt and studied the marks. Coyote!

What was a coyote doing so close to the yard? Tucker never allowed the pesky varmints anywhere near—

Tucker had gone with Riley this afternoon.

Andi swallowed and looked around. The tracks led straight for the henhouse. A sigh of relief came from her lungs. The coyote was after the chickens, not Jasper. Besides, a well-grown lamb was too big to be coyote fodder. Maybe.

Andi didn't wait for supper to talk to Riley. She nabbed him the minute he rode into the yard. "Jasper's gone, and there's coyote tracks all over the place."

Riley's brow furrowed. "I'll make sure Tucker stays close to home from now on. Do you think the coyote tracks have anything to do with Jasper's disappearance?"

Andi shook her head. "The tracks circled the henhouse and headed west. Besides, I would have heard bleating if the coyote went after Jasper." She shrugged. "No hens are missing either."

Riley found his rifle and headed out to search for Jasper. "I'll find him," he assured Andi with a smile. "Then we can have supper."

An hour later, Riley was back.

Andi was sitting in the rocking chair, sewing a few baby items. She dropped everything into the basket and looked up when Riley entered the room. "You didn't find Jasper," she whispered.

"Actually, I did," Riley said softly.

Andi's throat went dry. "Do you mean . . ."

Riley nodded. "I'm afraid so, darling. It looks like the coyote dragged Jasper off. All I found were a few tufts of wool and plenty of tracks."

Andi's heart broke. She was a rancher's daughter and now a rancher's wife. She'd had her share of heartbreak. Taffy's horrible passing three years ago was at the top of her list of sorrows. Wolves sometimes killed a newborn calf or a foal. Coyotes and foxes occasionally ran off with a hen.

Yes, she'd seen it all.

"It's the way this fallen world is, honey," big brother Justin always told Andi when he found her sobbing over some little pet that had died. She should have grown used to it by now.

She hadn't.

Andi looked down at her lap. Jasper had worn her out to the point where she wanted him gone. But not this way!

"Are you all right?" Riley asked.

Andi shrugged. It hurt, but she controlled her tears.

"I'm sorry he's gone," Riley said. "I know he was the lamb you always wanted."

Not really.

"He was proving to be too much work and trouble for me," Andi whispered before she could bite the words back. "I wanted to get rid of him. But I didn't want him to die." She raised her head.

"You wanted to let Jasper go?" Riley's hazel gaze bored into Andi's.

She nodded. "Caring for a lamb didn't turn out like I thought it would. Jasper was more trouble than he was fun. With only a couple weeks left until the baby arrives, I've been too worn out to enjoy him."

Andi swallowed. "I was even beginning to resent him." How awful did *that* sound?

"Why didn't you tell me?"

Andi bit her lip. "I saw how much fun you were having with Jasper. You really liked him."

"I did like him," Riley admitted. "But you mean more to me than a thousand lambs, Andi. You know that."

"I know. But—"

"But nothing." Riley snorted. "If keeping Jasper meant more worry and distress for you, I'm glad he's gone." He pulled Andi up from the rocking chair and hugged her.

She pondered. She should have told him sooner. Riley would have returned Jasper to Sadie, and Andi would be blissfully ignorant of her little lamb's fate.

Riley kissed the top of her head. "Jasper is gone, but I think it would be best to keep this to ourselves. Chad would never let you live down the fact that he was right about that pesky little lamb all along."

Andi cringed. *That's for sure!*

Baby Prescott let out a sudden kick that jerked Andi from her thoughts and took her breath away.

Riley noticed. "We'll have our own precious little lamb soon enough, sweetheart."

Riley was right about that.

She smiled up at him. "You can be sure I'll take good care of *this* lamb," she promised him. "Or my name's not Andrea Rose Carter Prescott."

ELEVEN

ANDI HAD A LITTLE LAMB

MEMORY CREEK RANCH, CALIFORNIA, JULY 4, 1887
Note: Giving birth in the 1880s (or during any time in history)
was risky. Readers can be grateful we live in modern times,
when having a baby carries much less risk.

I've had some memorable Fourth of Julys in my life, but this year's Fourth has turned out to be the most memorable of them all.

Chapter 1

Andi hoped and prayed Baby Prescott would make his or her appearance by June 30.

That didn't happen. Instead, she lost Jasper, her little lamb. If truth be told, however, Andi didn't have time to shed tears. She was too busy being miserable.

July in California is always *hot*. July first entered with a heat wave that tempted Andi to sit down fully clothed in what remained of Memory Creek. Worse, this baby was proving to be as stubborn as his mama.

Andi wanted this all over with before the Fourth of July. Visions of birthing this baby and showing him (or her) off in town at the Independence Day celebration swirled around inside her head.

If Mother ever got wind of this silly idea, she would have

forbidden her daughter to do such a foolish thing, even if Andi was grown up and married.

Which is why Andi never breathed a word of her intentions to her mother.

When the Fourth of July dawned hot—and no baby had made his appearance—Andi was determined to go into town to see the parade.

Riley was just as determined that she stay home. "My head spins thinking about what would happen if I let you do such a fool thing. You are much too close to your time. Your mother would have my hide hung out to dry."

Probably true, Andi conceded.

Besides, even if she did defy Riley, how would she get to town? Andi had lent Shasta to Mitch so he could win the race. Worse, she did feel kind of lousy this morning.

So, she gave in.

Mid-morning, Andi stood on the porch and watched the ranch hands gallop away for the festivities in town. She was more than a little envious. Riley had given all three of the men the rest of the day off.

She bit her lip, thinking about everything she would miss today: the speeches, the fireworks, the sideshows, and the horse races.

Especially the horse races.

Mitch was competing again this year. More than anything, Andi wanted to be in the audience with the baby in her arms, cheering for him and Shasta.

Now I'll miss it all. Andi sighed and entered the house. Tears pricked the inside of her eyelids. *Dirty darn.* She was so tired of carrying this baby around.

"Don't look so glum, Andi." Riley had donned an apron and was washing the breakfast dishes.

"Easy for you to say," she snapped. "You're not the one lugging this extra weight around."

Riley smiled. "You should be glad."

Andi cocked an eyebrow. "Whatever for?"

"For a husband like me." He wrinkled his nose. "Men don't usually do women's work, you know. Washing dishes is *definitely* women's work."

"You don't say!" Andi giggled. He did look funny in that red-checked apron and with suds up to his elbows.

Riley rinsed the last dish and reached for a towel. "I want you to take it easy today. Read a book or sew or something."

"Read or *sew*?" Andi shook her head. "No thanks."

"Then take a nap."

"I'm not sleepy. For goodness' sake, Riley! I want to do something fun today. Especially since I can't go into town." She grimaced. "Maybe I'll take a walk before the heat sucks me dry."

"Wait a minute and I'll go with you."

Andi pulled on her hat and knotted the stampede string. "You don't need to hover over me. I'm fine."

"I feel like a walk too."

Sure he did. So he could fuss over Andi like an old aunt. "Hurry up then."

"Hold your horses. I'm almost finished."

Riley swept the towel over the remaining plate, tucked it away in the cabinet, and wrung out the towel. "I've got to check something in the barn, and then we can take that walk."

Andi let out an impatient breath. "Fine. I'll meet you down at the creek. We can go wading. How about that? My feet are so hot and swollen, it would feel mighty good."

Riley smiled and plopped his hat on his head. "Great."

He headed for the door. "Maybe splashing too. Good idea."

It didn't take Andi long to walk to the creek. Or what was left of it. The spring rush was well over, but a good-sized trickle remained. It was enough to dip her toes in.

Andi carefully lowered herself to the ground. The dry, golden grass prickled through her skirt. *Ouch.* She wiggled back and forth to find a comfortable spot.

Now, for her high-topped shoes. She bit her lip. It was tricky work trying to take off her shoes. She could barely reach them. Andi huffed and puffed then fell backward in exhaustion.

Where was Riley when she needed him? He could be useful pulling off her boots.

I can do this! I got them on this morning. I can take them off. She loosened the buttons and reached for her boot toe.

With no warning, a stabbing pain ripped across Andi's belly. "Ow!" She gasped. "That really hurt. I guess I shouldn't have leaned over so hard." She patted her belly. "Sorry, sweet little one. I'll be more careful next time."

Which only goes to show how ignorant Andi was.

A few days before, Mother had ridden over. She seemed worried about Andi, just a little, and wanted to have that all-important mother-daughter talk about what to expect when it was time for the baby to make an appearance.

She'd asked if Andi had felt any pains yet. Not a twinge.

Mother smiled and assured her that if Andi did have belly aches over the next few days, it was nothing to worry about. It only meant her body was getting ready for the real work.

"But when you do have pains, send for me," she'd ended the conversation. "I'm happy to stay for a week or more. One just never knows."

Another shooting pain cut across Andi's belly, taking her breath away. What in the world was—

Her eyes widened as the pieces fell together. These must be those practice pains Mother had warned her about. She relaxed, then shuddered. If these were the practice pains, what would the *real* pains feel like?

"Andi!" Riley called, running up. "How's the water?"

Andi didn't answer. She gave him a look that must have scared him, for he dropped down beside her.

"What's wrong?"

Andi shook her head. "I don't know. I think I'm having some birthing pains."

Riley caught his breath.

"Mother says they're only practice ones, though," she reassured him. "When the men return from the celebration, you should probably send one of them to the ranch." She licked her lips and took a deep breath. "Because . . . I think I want my mother."

Another pain—stronger this time—gripped her, and she sucked in her breath.

"Andi!"

"It's all right." She blew out. "I got caught by surprise."

"No, it's *not* all right." Riley shook his head. He looked shaken. "I'm going for your mother right now."

Andi grabbed his hand. "Oh, no, you're not. You can't leave me here all alone. These might be practice pains like Mother says, but they hurt mighty bad."

Was Mother wrong? Could these be the real thing? Could Andi be having the baby now? Today? She gripped Riley's finger's tighter.

Riley rose and gently lifted Andi to her feet. "Well, the least I can do is make you comfortable. We're going inside. Our walk is over."

Andi agreed. Something was wrong. This was too fast. And

too painful to be practice *anything*. Her heart raced, but she took another deep breath and calmed herself.

"Even if the baby *is* on the way, first babies take at least a day or more to come," she said. "Mother told me so. People aren't like a mare or a cow. A mare might foal in an hour or two. Sometimes faster."

Andi managed a weak smile at her mother's words from last week. *"Justin took all day and all night to come,"* she'd told Andi. *"And do you remember Lucy's first?"*

Andi had shaken her head. She was only a young girl back then. She knew nothing about babies—only foals and calves. One day Lucy was in the family way. The next time Andi saw her, Sammy was a swaddled bundle on her lap.

Lucy made it look easy.

"Andi, what should we do?"

Riley's worried question yanked Andi back to the here and now. She pondered. What to do? If babies took all day, then maybe Riley did have time to fetch Mother.

She was ready to let him go when another pain hit. It came awfully close to the one before it. By the time she got back to the house, she knew.

I am really and truly about to have the baby.

Then a worse thought hit her. If she'd skipped all those "practice" pains that come and go a week or two ahead of the real event, then might this baby decide he or she was not going to wait a full day and night? Even if it was the first?

No! Please not today. Not when Mother's in town. Not when there's no one here besides Riley to fetch her or to go for Dr. Weaver.

Pleading with herself did not work. Not even clenching her fists worked.

Baby Prescott was coming, and there was nothing Andi could

do about it. When her water broke with the next pain, Andi knew she was stuck. Really stuck.

And she was scared to death.

Chapter 2

Mr. Dickens' opening lines of A Tale of Two Cities came to mind today. "It was the best of times. It was the worst of times." This day started out as the worst of times.

R iley!" Andi hollered. Nothing hurt at the moment, but her fear had soared to mountain heights. The thought of being alone, with no mother and no doctor—and no easy way to fetch them and bring them here—threatened to suffocate her.

Riley came running into the bedroom, where he'd settled Andi only a few minutes before. "What's wrong?"

"This baby is really and truly coming."

His face turned ashen. "Are you sure, sweetheart? Are you *really* sure?" He sat down on the bed.

Oh, yes, Andi was sure. When her water broke, she knew she had passed the point of no return. She shivered in the heat. Before she could say anything, another pain exploded inside. Thankfully, it was short . . . for now.

"What are we going to do, Riley?"

He sprang up from the bed. His eyes were wide with panic. "I don't know, I don't know." He ran his fingers through his hair and began to pace.

"You've got to help me." Andi struggled to stay calm. "I don't know what to do."

"I don't either!" he cried out. "I'm just the father. Fathers don't have babies. Doctors and women help the mothers."

"Dr. Weaver and Mother aren't here," Andi said. "You *have* to help me."

He shook his head. "I'll ride Dakota lickety-split and get the doctor and your mother." He paused in his pacing. "Didn't your mother say first babies take their time? I've got plenty of time to get to town and back. Three hours. Not a moment longer. I promise."

Three hours? Was he crazy? Andi couldn't do this alone for three hours. She was too frightened. What if the baby came while he was gone?

Nothing had gone according to plan. Mother had told Andi the pains start quietly, gradually, sometimes only one every half hour or so. That gave everybody time to get things ready. Then the pains slowly got shorter and harder.

Mother was wrong! These pains had started with as much of a bang as a Fourth of July rocket, and they probably would not fade away anytime soon. No, they would only get worse.

What a horrifying thought!

"The only promise you're going to make is that you won't leave me alone!" Andi yelled at him.

"Then . . . what?" He approached the bed.

Andi reached out and grabbed his hand. "There's no choice. You're the only one here. You have to help me birth this baby."

Riley's face reflected his reluctance and anxiety, but he set his jaw and nodded. "All right. Tell me what to do."

Andi had no idea. She was not experienced with birthing babies. She only knew what to do if a mare was foaling.

Hmmm, could it be similar?

Another pain convinced Andi that having a baby was nothing like a mare foaling. She wracked her brain for anything. Any idea at all. "Boil some water," she ordered.

Somewhere in her memory she remembered something that had to do with water. And string. "Boil some string to tie off the baby's cord. Uh . . . and throw the scissors in there too. You need it to cut the cord."

Andi didn't think Riley's face could get any paler. She was wrong. All color left it.

A pain ripped through her. "Do it!"

That got him running.

When the pain subsided, Andi felt terrible for yelling at her sweet husband. But she was scared too. She'd heard about young mothers *dying* when they had a baby.

Hot tears sprang to her eyes. She didn't want to die. Not because she was afraid of where she was going after death, but she didn't want to leave Riley and the baby. *Please, God, make me brave.*

Right now, Andi felt about five years old. She wanted her mother more than at any other time of her life.

When Riley returned, he was carrying a cup of tea. *Tea?*

"I heard your mother telling you that raspberry tea helps with the delivery." He gave Andi a lopsided grin. "And boy, do we need all the help we can get."

She was between the knife-like pains at that moment, so she laughed and grabbed his hand. "Stay here and talk to me."

So, he did. Riley's stories helped Andi to get through the pains that—sure as shooting—were coming closer together and lasting longer than either she or Riley wanted them too.

What seemed like hours later, Andi chanced a glance at the bedside clock. It was only a little past noon. *It's only been a couple of hours?*

This was no fun at all.

All of a sudden, Andi wanted to get up. She wanted to do

something—anything—that would take her mind off all this pain and uncertainty.

Riley pitched a fit when she told him. "No, you'd better stay in bed."

Andi shook her head. She was determined to get up.

Riley sighed and gave in.

For a wonder, walking around really helped. Andi even felt the baby shift and settle in. When a pain started, she paused and concentrated with all her might to not crumple into a trembling ball of terror and hurt.

"I think you may just wear a path on the rug," Riley joked as they walked around the braided rug in the sitting room.

Andi looked up.

He winked. "Walking is better. You made the right choice. Maybe it will speed things up."

Riley clearly wanted this over with as much as Andi did.

She knew she looked ghastly. Sweat poured down her forehead. She'd shed her dress an hour ago and exchanged it for the loosest cotton nightgown she owned. It didn't help.

The afternoon got longer and hotter. Riley fanned Andi's face, but all it did was move the oppressive heat around. She finally collapsed back into bed. "I'm too tired and too hurting to walk one more step."

Everything went downhill after that. For sure, a Southern Pacific railroad engine was running over the top of her. "I don't think I can do this."

Riley rubbed her back. "But you *are* doing it, darling."

"What if . . . what if the baby never comes?"

Riley shook his head. "It's only been five hours. Five short hours."

There was nothing short about five hours.

"But it *hurts!*" Her last word trailed off into loud wailing.

She couldn't help it. The pain would not let up.

Andi clenched her teeth to keep from shrieking the next time a pain overwhelmed her. She groaned and prayed, and downed two cups of raspberry tea, but nothing seemed to help.

At last, as the pains continued to grip her with increasing speed and discomfort, she finally gave up. It was no use. Everything hurt too much. She couldn't be brave or quiet any longer.

"Nobody but the horses can hear you," Riley assured her. He smiled. "And me. I think you should yell as loud as you want. Especially if it helps."

It did help. A little.

When the sun shone its last rays through the west window, Andi knew she'd been at this most of the day. One thing was certain. There was no more horrible way to spend a day than this.

Then a new kind of pain overwhelmed her. The need to push. "I want Mother," she whimpered.

What was it about mothers and daughters? Andi loved Riley. He was her sweet husband, and he was doing something far removed from his normal life.

Mother, though, would know exactly what to do to help the pain. She would know exactly what to tell Andi to help birth this baby into the world.

Riley knew nothing except that he'd better not move one step away.

"It'll all be worth it soon," Riley crooned. He brushed the hair away from her sweaty face. "You're doing great. Don't focus on the pain. Just keep thinking about the baby."

Andi rolled the words around in her head. Don't focus on the pain? Was he kidding? "Easy for you to say."

"Lord, help Andi do this," Riley prayed suddenly. "For the

baby. For her. For me."

Riley's prayer calmed Andi. Yes, he was right. She must focus on the baby, not the pain. "How much longer?" she pleaded.

"Not much longer."

Andi drew a deep, shuddering breath. When the next pain came, she pushed even harder. She couldn't help it. She had no choice. When the pain receded, she rested.

If only I could drop into a deep, dreamless sleep and wake up with the baby in my arms.

The next pain convinced her that was not going to happen. She clenched Riley's hand in a bone-gripping grasp. "I . . . can't . . . do this!"

"Yes, you can," he said firmly. But his expression, no matter how hard he might be trying to cover it, spoke the truth. Riley was scared half out of his wits. "Please, Andi. I love you. Don't give up. Please don't."

The desperate, pleading look in Riley's eyes sent a fresh wave of determination through Andi. As the pain subsided, she managed a tiny smile. "All right. I love you too."

With lightning speed, another horrible pain ripped through her body, the worse yet. She gritted her teeth and prayed the only two words that came to mind. *Lord, help.* Then she pushed with all her might.

A minute later, Andi heard a baby's thin, high wailing, and the pain was gone. As much as she wanted to see her baby, she was too tired. She sank into a blessed sleep.

***

"Andi, wake up."

She opened her eyes. Riley was standing by her bedside.

Her mind felt fuzzy, full of cotton. *Where am I? What happened?*

It came to her like a bolt of lightning. "The baby!" She tried to sit up.

"Hold your horses." Riley gently pushed Andi back onto the pillows. "You need to take it easy." He tucked the covers around her. "Our son is fine."

"Son?" Andi's heart squeezed with joy. "We have a boy?"

Riley reached into the cradle and drew out a squirming bundle. The baby was wrapped in a light blanket.

Andi's breath caught. Her heart throbbed. She held out shaky hands, hardly believing it was true. No words came.

But her tears came. Tears of overpowering wonder and joy.

Riley put the baby into Andi's arms. She choked. "Oh, Riley. He's beautiful."

"He's got all his fingers and toes," Riley said, chuckling. "I checked."

Riley had done more than check for fingers and toes. He'd tied off the cord and wiped the baby off. A wisp of fine, dark hair covered his tiny head.

Andi snuggled him close. Suddenly, all the pain and hard work seemed a thing of the ancient past. Gone, never to be remembered.

It was all worth it. She touched the tiny, wrinkled hand that peeped out from the blanket and placed a gentle kiss on his head. *I'd do it all over again in a heartbeat.*

The happy tears continued to stream from Andi's eyes. She looked up. "He's *ours*, Riley."

Ever since Samuel had been born to Lucy and Justin, Andi had discovered a special love for babies. But *nothing* compared with the love she felt for this little person.

Riley ran gentle fingers over the baby's fuzz of hair. "Our very own Jared Riley Prescott."

A bubble of laughter rose up in Andi's throat. "Jasper was

no lamb compared to *this* little lamb."

Riley nodded and reached for the baby. "You've been through a lot. You need to get some rest."

Andi shook her head and cuddled the baby closer. "No."

Nobody, not even the baby's father, was going to take Jared away from her. She'd worked long and hard to earn the privilege of holding him for as long as she liked.

He started to squirm. Then he let out a loud wail.

"Besides," Andi reasoned, "he's hungry, and only I can take care of that." She gave Riley an impish grin. She was feeling one hundred percent better.

Riley backed away. "The ranch hands should be home in another hour or so. Night has fallen, and the fireworks should be about over. When they get back, I'll send one of them to the Circle C for your mother."

"Sure." Andi snuggled with the baby.

"I also want Doc Weaver to look you over," Riley said. "To make sure I did a good job as a midwife. He needs to check the baby too."

Andi nodded. *Yes, you do that,* her sleepy thoughts said. She closed her eyes. *Thank you, Lord, for a husband like Riley. And for this beautiful gift.*

True, this day had begun as "the worst of times." It had surely ended, however, as "the best of times."

TWELVE

RILEY PRESCOTT—PROUD PAPA

MEMORY CREEK RANCH, CALIFORNIA, JULY 4-5, 1887

All the pain and terror dissolved like morning dew the minute Jared was born. But that night was not over yet. When the clock chimed midnight, the ranch hands were still not back. Riley was starting to pace.

Riley had promised to fetch Andi's mother the minute the Memory Creek ranch hands rode in. Trouble was, they didn't ride in.

The clock chimed ten o'clock. Then eleven o'clock.

When the clock struck midnight, Riley looked fit to be tied. He stomped into the bedroom, where Andi lay half-asleep. Jared was curled up in her arms. He'd fallen asleep eating.

Andi sighed. It felt good just to doze and cuddle him.

Riley woke her up with a start. "I'm going to fire them all— every last man," he growled. He thrust the lace curtains aside and peered down the road. "Why can't they come back on time for once?"

Andi knew he couldn't see a thing.

"Riley," she said softly, so as not to startle the baby. "How were they supposed to know you needed them? Go easy. It's the Fourth of July."

Now that things were over, Andi was the calm one.

Riley ran a shaky hand through his brown tangles. "Uh-uh. It's July fifth now. The clock chimed midnight."

He shook his head and began pacing. "You need your mother, or the doctor, or . . . *anybody* but me."

Andi wrinkled her forehead, puzzled. The worst was surely over. What was eating Riley? "Get some sleep. I'm going to." Her head felt full of cotton.

Instead of coming to bed, he sat down next to Andi and gave her a worried look. "Are you *sure* you're all right?"

Andi shrugged. "Just tired. Why?"

Riley's voice trembled. "I never told you this, mostly because I didn't want to worry you. My mother's sister had a baby a long time ago. I was just a boy."

He took one of Andi's hands and squeezed. "Everything went well, at least that's what Mama told me when she came home from Aunt Sophie's house. 'A little girl, Riley,' she told me. 'You have a cousin.'"

"I wasn't all that excited about babies at the time," Riley said. "I was eleven, and girl cousins were even less exciting."

He paused before going on. "Mama had helped Aunt Sophie with the birthing, but the next day when she checked on her sister, something was very wrong."

Andi caught her breath. "What?"

"Mama came running into our little house at Fort Laramie and shouted for Pa to ride to the closest town and fetch a doctor for Sophie," Riley said. "Mama was hysterical. I cowered in the corner. Even at the ripe old age of eleven, I knew something terrible was happening."

Riley shuddered. "Long story short. Aunt Sophie started bleeding. Something had gone wrong inside, and even Mama didn't know how to help."

A sob choked Riley's throat. "By the time Pa got back with the doctor, it was too late. Aunt Sophie had died." He shook his head. "Baby Sarah lived, but it was hard on Uncle Joseph."

Riley squeezed Andi's hand until she felt like the blood would be cut off. "That can't happen to you, Andi. It just can't." He jumped up and looked out the window again.

Andi bit her lip. She had gotten up once since Jared was born. She had barely made it to the chamber pot and back to bed before keeling over. How much blood was too much?

Maybe Riley was right to be concerned. "Ride over to the ranch," she whispered. "Bring back Mother. She'll know if everything is all right or not."

Fear had suddenly gripped Andi.

Riley hurried over. "I don't want to leave you, but by the time those dolts get back and I turn them around to ride for the Circle C, I could be there and back."

"I promise I'll lie right here," Andi said. "I won't move a muscle. I'm so tired that I'll probably fall asleep."

Riley bent over and kissed Andi's forehead. He brushed his fingers across Jared's tiny head and bolted from the room.

The last thing Andi heard was Dakota's hooves pounding down the driveway. A glow passed the window on his way.

Andi smiled. At least he'd remembered to light a lantern. It was black as ink outside. She couldn't remember when the moon would be up, or if it would rise at all tonight.

"Please watch over Riley," she prayed quietly.

Then she fell asleep.

***

Andi woke with a start. Jared was still sleeping. Riley was banging through the front door.

A soft but firm voice scolded him. "Riley, shh!"

Andi saw lights being lit in the other room. Her own lamp was dim, but she could make out the time: one-thirty.

She smiled sleepily. Riley had made good time.

Then Mother stepped through the doorway.

For the first time since Andi could remember, her mother looked in a dither. Her hair was amiss, and she was pulling off her riding cloak without worrying where to toss it.

"Oh, Andrea!" Then she turned and spoke to Riley in her better-be-quick-about-it voice. "The basket. Bring it in here."

Poor Mother! Andi felt better already. "Hello, Mother," she greeted her softly.

"Oh, my darling!" She sat down on the bed and wrapped her arms around Andi. "What a time you must have had." She peeked over at Jared but made no move to pick him up.

"You first. Then I'll admire my grandson." She smiled, but it looked forced.

Riley set the wicker basket on the floor.

Mother's capable hands rummaged through the basket. She took out two small tin canisters and thrust them at Riley. "Boil some water and brew these herbs." She paused. "And be quick about it."

Riley took off to do her bidding.

Then Mother turned back to Andi. "I've brought ginger and motherwort. Motherwort is the important one. We want your womb to contract and return to normal as quickly as possible."

Andi made a face. The herb she remembered gagging on was ginger, in the form of tea. Cook had made her drink it one morning on the cattle drive, when she'd keeled over.

"Herbs make me sick, Mother."

"You will thank me," Mother said. "If your womb lies flaccid, you could bleed too much."

Andi's throat tightened. She'd seen the blood earlier. Was it too much? She suddenly wanted to drink a gallon of the nasty stuff, especially after hearing Riley's story.

"When was the baby born?" Mother asked while Riley banged around in the kitchen.

Andi paused, then shook her head. "I don't remember. I didn't think to look at the clock. Late evening? The sun wasn't shining through the window any longer. It was dark."

Mother nodded. "It hasn't been too long then." She sighed. "I can't believe I went to town today! I should have ridden over and checked on you or stayed with you."

She smiled and patted Andi's arm. "I know you wanted to see the celebration."

Missing the Fourth of July celebration was the furthest thing from Andi's mind right now.

Riley brought the tea just then. Andi sniffed it and knew right away it was going to be a nasty drink. But she choked it down—every last drop. Her stomach clenched, and the brew nearly came back up.

Mother rose and looked around. Apparently satisfied by what she found, she relaxed. "You got up?"

Andi nodded. "But I thought I would faint, so I went right back to bed."

"I think everything will be all right, but honestly!" She chuckled. "You never fail to surprise me." Her earlier fear and worry were erased from her face.

Apparently, Andi would be fine. *Thank You, God.*

Having a baby seemed more complicated after the birth than during it.

Mother sent Riley back to the kitchen for more herb tea. Then she held out her arms toward the baby. "Now, let me take a peek at this little blessing."

Andi handed Jared over and lay back. *Mother is here. Everything will be fine.*

Mother laid out a blanket and unwrapped the baby from his coverings. She looked him over carefully, paying special attention to what was left of his cord.

A long, relieved sigh came from her throat. "Riley is a smart young man. It appears that he did everything right. Boiled the water?"

Andi nodded.

"Rinsed the scissor and the string?"

"Yes, I think so." To be honest, Andi didn't remember any of that. Riley had presented Jared to her, and she hadn't done anything since then but cuddle him.

Mother clucked her tongue, cleaned the baby up, and handed him back. By now, Jared was wailing.

"A good, strong cry," Mother said with approval. "He's clean and dry." She slumped into a nearby chair just as Riley returned with more tea.

Andi made a face but drank it.

Mother smiled up at her son-in-law. "I was scared half out of my mind when you came barging into the ranch house, Riley. I was just retiring and heard the shouting."

She turned to Andi. "I thought you were in labor and quickly got ready. Riley nearly dragged me out of the house. He'd already snagged Chad and asked him to hitch up the buggy."

"I reckon I was a little nervous," Riley admitted.

Mother laughed. "A *little* nervous? My goodness! You must be taking shouting lessons from Chad."

Riley gave her a tiny smile. "Now that you're here with Andi, I need to check on the stock. The cow is bawling her head off. I missed the evening milking, and the men are still gone."

"Oh, yes," Mother agreed. "Do what you need to do, Riley."

She turned back to Andi and finished her story. "We were halfway to your place when I finally figured out that you had already given birth. Riley told me then what happened—that he'd delivered the baby. Heavens, Andrea. All by himself!"

"Well, I helped a little." Andi smirked and tightened her hold on her precious bundle.

"Of course you did." Mother chuckled.

"I wouldn't let him go to town or anything," Andi said. "Everything happened so quickly." She looked at Mother. "Nothing happened like you told me. I was so scared." Tears pricked her eyelids. The memory was too recent.

Mother took Andi's hand. "God was surely with you and that young man. I'm proud of you both, and I'm sorry I wasn't here to help." She rose and turned down the lamp. "Good night, sweetheart. I'll sleep on the settee."

Andi yawned. Weariness overwhelmed her. What a lot of work it was to birth a baby! "Thank you for coming, Mother," she whispered. "I can *really* rest now."

"Don't worry about a thing, sweetheart. I'm going to stay all week. I'll look after Riley and take care of the housework and cooking for as long as you need me." She smiled. "I'll sneak in a minute or two occasionally to rock the baby too."

Peace and contentment flowed through Andi. Her eyelids fluttered. "Thank you, Mother. Good night."

What a wonderfully happy beginning to the next chapter of her life—being a mother. Andi fell asleep with a smile on her lips.

BOOKS BY SUSAN K. MARLOW
CircleCAdventures.com

Circle C Beginnings

Andi's Pony Trouble

Andi's Indian Summer

Andi's Fair Surprise

Andi's Scary School Days

Andi's Lonely Little Foal

Andi's Circle C Christmas

Circle C Stepping Stones

Andi Saddles Up

Andi Under the Big Top

Andi Lassos Trouble

Andi to the Rescue

Andi Dreams of Gold

Andi Far from Home

Circle C Adventures

ANDREA CARTER AND THE . . .

Long Ride Home

Dangerous Decision

Family Secret

San Francisco Smugglers

Trouble with Treasure

Price of Truth

Circle C Milestones

Thick as Thieves

Heartbreak Trail

The Last Ride

Courageous Love

Goldtown Beginnings

Jem Strikes Gold

Jem's Frog Fiasco

Jem and the Mystery Thief

Jem Digs Up Trouble

Jem and the Golden Reward

Jem's Wild Winter

Goldtown Adventures

Badge of Honor

Tunnel of Gold

Canyon of Danger

River of Peril

Made in USA - Kendallville, IN
1167458_9781728929248
12.14.2020 1328